BARLEY AND RYE
by Rebecca J. Carlson

The Adventure of Lost Castle
The Curses of Lost Forest
The Wizard of Frogsmire

BARLEY AND RYE
THE CURSES OF LOST FOREST

REBECCA J. CARLSON

Barley and Rye
The Curses of Lost Forest

ISBN 979-8-9864014-1-6 (paperback)
ISBN 979-8-9864014-3-0 (e-book)

Published by Far Away Books
55-568 Naniloa Loop #4A, Laie, Hawaii 96762

This novel is a work of fiction. Names, descriptions, entities, and
incidents included in the story are products of the author's
imagination. Any resemblance to actual persons, events, and
entities is entirely coincidental.

Cover by Rachel Bayles
Illustrations by Rachelle Hoffman

First published in the United States by Fiction Vortex

First Far Away Books Edition: November 2022

Published in the United States of America

For Ellie, who started me on a whole new adventure.

The Land Far Away

Lost Forest

Rose Grove Kingdom

Red Mountains

Troll Hollow

Frog Pond

Wizard's Keep

Witc Tow

The Fields of Sorrow

The Land Where Faerie Tales Dwell

Knight's Peak

Seaside Kingdom

Wistful Valle

Isle of Magic

Gloridian

Swo Tru

Flying Island

EPISODE ONE: SIR BARLEY FIELDS OF HUMBLE VILLAGE

ONE

Anyone would think Barley had defeated the Dragon of the Deep all by himself—the way he strutted around the village wearing his new sword, the one with the crest of the Royal Knights of the Land Far Away. That sword was too long for Barley, who still had some growing up to do. Everywhere Barley went, the tip of the sword's sheath trailed in the dirt. It got in the way when Barley tried to milk the cow or help mow the hay, but Barley wouldn't part with it for anything.

He had a letter too, signed by the king himself, making Barley the Lord Protector over Humble Village. Barley carried the letter tucked in his belt and showed it to whoever asked him, and even sometimes to those who didn't ask him. The villagers were all very impressed, but if they wanted to know exactly what the letter said, Barley couldn't tell them. Neither Barley nor anyone else in the village knew how to read.

Rye wasn't jealous of his younger brother Barley. No, not exactly. He only had this itchy feeling inside him, a feeling that he needed to do something, something all on his own, some brave deed that would earn him a place among the Royal Knights of the Land Far Away. Then he and Barley could be knights together.

But doing a brave deed would have to wait. Now was the time of harvest, and all hands were needed in the fields. There were apples to pick, turnips and carrots to dig and tuck away in the straw of the cool root cellar, winter rye to plant, and summer barley to cut and bundle.

Late one autumn morning, Barley and Rye worked near the road, cutting sweet, warm stalks of grain the same sunny yellow as Barley's hair. Mother followed behind them and bound the grain in bundles while Father stood the bundles in stacks to dry.

Rye gripped a handful of stalks and sliced them free with his sickle, then stood up to stretch his back. That's when he saw the wizard standing in the road, dressed in deep purple from the tip of his tall, pointed hat to the bottom of his robes. Rye had seen wizards pass through Humble Village before, but he'd never seen one stop.

"Now here is a very marvelous thing," the wizard said in a creaky voice, as if his throat was choked with the dust of old books. His eyes glittered with the same curiosity as those of the black-hooded, white-breasted magpie on his shoulder. "A farm boy with a knight's sword!"

"Good morning, master wizard!" Barley called.

"And a good morning to you!" the wizard said. "Pray tell me, lad. How did you come by that fine weapon?"

Barley jogged to the road. "I'm a knight. See?" He pulled the king's letter from his belt and handed it to the wizard.

Rye, who was trying very hard not to grin, stepped closer to Barley.

The wizard drew a pair of spectacles from inside his robes and placed them on the tip of his long nose. As he studied the paper in front of him, his peppery-gray eyebrows went down, and his forehead pinched in deep creases. He tipped his head to the side with a puzzled frown.

"Is something wrong?" Barley asked.

The wizard said, "I'm terribly sorry. There must be some mistake. This appears to be a rather outdated list of tariffs on imported goods."

"What?" Barley asked in disbelief.

The wizard read aloud, "Section Seventeen, Textiles. Flax, three coppers per bale. Silk, five coppers per skein. Cotton . . ."

"But that's not what it said at all!" Barley slapped his hand to his belt as if to see if there was another letter there. "The messenger read it to us in front of the king and everybody! It says I'm a knight, and it's my job to protect the village." He paced a small circle in the field, searching the ground until he came up short in front of Rye. "What are you grinning about?" he demanded.

Rye pulled another folded paper from his inside vest pocket, one that looked almost exactly like the one Barley had handed to the wizard.

"Is that—? Did you—?" Barley gasped and snatched the paper. "Rye! You switched letters on me!" His face turned red and furious. "When?"

Rye shrugged. "I found the other paper in a rubbish heap at the castle, but I didn't switch them until we were almost home. I was wondering when you'd notice."

"From a rubbish heap?" Barley shouted. "You mean to tell me I've been showing everyone 'Flax, three coppers per bale,' and telling them it was my letter from the king?" He took the list of tariffs from the wizard and held it next to the letter to compare them.

"No one knew the difference." Rye laughed and used his elbow to defend himself as Barley whacked at him with *Section Seventeen, Textiles.*

"Oh Rye, you rascal," Mother said. "Tell your brother you're sorry."

"I'm terribly sorry," Rye said, though he wasn't sorry at all. "Do you want the wizard to read your letter?"

"Yes," Barley said, still fuming. He handed the wizard the real letter. "Sorry about that, master wizard."

"No harm done," the wizard said with a half-smiling glance at Rye.

Even the magpie seemed interested in the letter. It leaned over and trained a bright, black eye on it. The wizard cleared his throat, but his voice came out as creaky as ever. "King Hugric, His Illustrious Majesty, sovereign over the Land Far Away, doth hereby declare . . ."

"Wait, wait!" Mother said. "I want the whole village to hear this."

TWO

Word that a wandering wizard would be reading Barley's letter from the king spread through the village. It wasn't long before a small crowd gathered around the well. While waiting for all the villagers to arrive, the wizard earned squealing laughs from the small children by pulling daisies or brightly colored beetles out of their ears.

"Everyone's here," Mother said as Soldier Jack came last to join the group.

"Couldn't start without me!" Soldier Jack said proudly. "I was the one who taught Sir Barley how to fight."

Rye smiled as he remembered Soldier Jack's lessons, which mostly consisted of the old soldier sleeping under a tree while Barley and Rye fought each other with their toy wooden swords.

The wizard fed the last beetle to his magpie. He coughed loudly, and when the crowd fell silent, he began to read. "King Hugric, His Illustrious Majesty, sovereign over the Land Far Away, doth hereby declare that Sir Barley Fields, vanquisher of the Dragon of the Deep, shall henceforth, and with all his heirs after him, be Lord Protector over Humble

Village and the lands roundabout, even unto the borders of the Lost Forest on the east, west, and south, with the village on the northernmost bound."

Mother gasped, and Father gave Barley a solid thump on the shoulder.

"He shall also be permitted to erect one castle for the defense of his lands in a location of his choosing, for which we have provided him with three bags of gold to hire workmen and craftsmen for the task."

Barley gave Rye a baffled look as if he had forgotten it would be his job to build a castle. Maybe he expected a fairy would come along and make his castle magically appear overnight.

"As a knight of the Land Far Away, Sir Barley Fields shall be responsible to quell all unpeaceable activity of giants, dragons, demons, trolls, brigands, outlaws, and other enemies to the crown that are found within his borders. He shall also be responsible, in time of war, to report to the royal army with a number of soldiers enlisted from among the inhabitants of his lands. Lastly, he shall be responsible for collecting taxes, to the total sum of ten gold pieces per year and remitting them to the royal tax collector."

"Taxes!" the villagers cried out in dismay. No one in Humble Village had paid taxes for as long as anyone could remember.

"Don't worry!" Barley said. "I can pay the taxes out of the gold the king gave me."

"If you have any gold left after building the castle," Rye said.

"Oh, right." Barley frowned, then brightened up. "I'm sure it won't cost that much to build a castle. We'll build a small one. How about that?"

THREE

The villagers went back to their work, muttering about interfering kings and taxes. They glanced suspiciously at the sky, as if there might be unpeaceable giants or dragons ready to descend on them now that there was a knight for them to quarrel with.

The wizard asked, "Sir Barley Fields, please do tell me how a very young . . . knight like yourself managed to defeat the mighty Dragon of the Deep." The magpie hopped down to the cuff of the wizard's dark purple sleeve and peered at Barley.

"I didn't. It was Rye who tricked the dragon," Barley said. "He tricked him into promising not to trouble the Emerald Realms ever again. Isn't that right, Rye?"

Rye nodded as a heavy sadness wrapped around him. It wasn't fair. If driving the Lord of Lost Castle and all his brigands out of the forest had been enough for Barley to be knighted, then banishing the Dragon of the Deep from the Emerald Realms should have been enough for Rye to earn the same honor.

"So then why does this say . . ." The wizard frowned at the letter while the magpie on his wrist clacked its beak.

"That's a long story," Rye said.

"I'm not in a hurry," the wizard said.

It was almost midday, so Mother Fields invited the wizard to their cottage for a meal. While they walked, Barley told the story of last summer's adventures, how Barley rescued Rye from the brigands of Lost Forest with the help of a witch and a magic sword, and then how Rye rescued Barley from the Dragon of the Deep with the help of a knight named Sir Pinsky and a friendly selkie boy.

"Remarkable," the wizard said as Barley finished the story. "So the king decreed that Sir Barley should be known for defeating the dragon so that your friend, Sir Pinsky, could wield the magic sword on his behalf?"

Rye sighed. "Yes. It didn't matter in the end that Sir Pinsky didn't defeat the dragon. The king's decree stands."

The wizard chuckled in his throat and put a gentle hand on Rye's shoulder. "Why so sad, young Rye? You're not done yet, are you? Befriending magical creatures and outwitting dragons already? I expect we'll be hearing more from you, my boy. Mark my words!"

Rye hoped it was true. He hoped someday everyone would be hearing that he'd been made a knight. He hoped it so hard, it hurt.

FOUR

At the doorway of the cottage, the wizard took off his hat and ducked inside.

"Welcome to our home, master wizard," Father said. "Pardon, but I don't think we asked your name."

"I am the Good Wizard Thornberry. Not to be confused with the Bad Wizard Thornberry. He's no relation of mine, unless it's a very distant one. I've asked him to change his name multiple times, but he absolutely refuses. At any rate, I am the Good Wizard Thornberry of Wizard's Keep, and I am on my way home after a very successful tour of the countryside in which I have banished two demons, collected a few rare potion ingredients, and discovered a fantastic new spell for waterproofing boots. I'm very pleased to make your acquaintance, Farmer Fields and family."

While Mother sliced bread and Father fried up sausages, Barley asked the Good Wizard Thornberry to read the king's letter once more. As the wizard read, Barley took a piece of cold, charred wood from the fireplace and scratched drawings on the stones of the hearth. He drew a clump of huts surrounded by a wide ring of trees, then a rough castle with crooked walls and towers sprouting out of it. Below that came an angry giant, a flying dragon, and some scraggly monsters with extra heads, arms, and tails. On the next stone, he scratched out an army of stick men, a sword, and a crown. Last of all, he made ten circles for the ten gold pieces he owed the king for his yearly taxes.

"There!" Barley said. "Now I should be able to remember everything."

After everyone had enjoyed a good meal and Wizard Thornberry stood up to go, Barley said, "No, wait! We should pay you for reading the letter." He dashed up the ladder to the loft and came down with a gold piece in his hand.

The wizard held up his hands. "That's far too much, Sir Barley. I would be in your debt."

"No, please," Barley said. "Take it!"

"Very well. If you insist," said the wizard. "But remember, I owe you a service. If you should ever need my assistance, you'll find me at Wizard's Keep, and if you don't find me there, my fellow wizards will be glad to help you."

Before he left, the Good Wizard Thornberry cast his waterproofing spell on all the boots in the house. Then, with his magpie and his hat, he continued south on the road to Wizard's Keep.

FIVE

The very next day, Father Fields took Barley to Oakbridge Crossing to hire workmen for the castle. When they returned, Barley chose a low hill overlooking the White River and showed the workmen where to dig foundations for the walls. All the villagers helped haul white stones up from the riverbed. Every day that fall, from the first light of dawn until the last gray of dusk, Barley and Rye were either harvesting or working to build the castle.

As hard as he worked and as weary as he was, Rye found time every night to sit by the fire and study the king's letter. Rye had been impressed by the wizard's ability to read, and he wanted to learn to do it for himself. Using Barley's pictures to help him, he tried to match the writing on the paper with the words he remembered. With a piece of charcoal from the fire, he copied the words in the letter onto the hearth, sweeping the stones clean and starting from the beginning over and over. It gave him something to do other than wish he could set out right away on an adventure of his own. It was too late in the season to think of traveling.

By the time the snows came, the walls of Barley's castle stood only knee high. The workmen were dismissed and told to come back in the spring. The harvest had been good that year, so Humble Village passed the winter cozy and content. Barley's castle was almost forgotten under its deep snowy blanket. Barley and Rye found that their magically water-proofed boots kept their feet wonderfully warm and dry as they trudged through the snow to feed the sheep and the cows and then dashed off for sledding and snowball fights with their friends.

The boots were also very nice to have that one moonlit night when Rye, with Barley's willing help, crept out and built a pack of snow wolves belly-creeping toward the sheep-fold. Their work was convincing enough that when Father went out just before dawn the next morning he shouted loud enough to wake half the village. He knocked the head off one of the wolves with a bucket before he realized they were only made of snow. For the rest of the week, Barley and Rye had to do all their father's chores as well as their own. Both boys agreed it had been worth it.

When the snow began to melt and the river broke out of its icy bonds, the castle workmen returned. Many of them brought their families, and with Barley's permission, they built new cottages along the village road for themselves. The village seemed to be growing faster than the castle.

With the warmer weather, Rye began to think of leaving home, and how to tell his family he was leaving, and what direction he might go to find a brave deed to do so he could become a Knight of the Land Far Away. Most of all, he wondered if Barley could get along without him while he was gone. Barley's life would be so dull without an older brother to tease him and get him into trouble all the time.

One night, Rye sat by the fire and wrote the king's letter from memory on the stones of the hearth while Barley sat at the kitchen table, counting his gold. Barley made small piles of coins and pushed them around until finally he shoved himself back from the table.

"I'll never be able to finish the castle!" Barley said. "Look! The gold's over half gone, and the walls aren't nearly half as high as they should be, and then there's the taxes!" He slumped down in his seat. "Rye, I thought you said being a knight was all about going around and having adventures and slaying dragons and such. How can I go on an adventure when I have castles and taxes to worry about?"

"You want to go on more adventures?" Rye asked. Barley was already a knight, famous for driving off brigands, which he had done, and for defeating a dragon, which he hadn't. Rye was the one who needed to go on an adventure so he could be knighted too.

"Of course!" Barley said. "Adventures are like sausage pies. You have one, and you think you're done, but the next day, you find you're wanting another."

"I was thinking . . ." Rye began. He had been going to say that maybe once the castle was done, they could go out adventuring together, but Rye didn't want to wait that long. Besides, he wanted to go by himself. If he didn't, how could he be sure that whatever brave deed he did would be his alone?

Barley had gone back to grumbling and pushing his gold coins around, so that was the end of the conversation.

SIX

The next morning, after Barley and Rye finished their chores, they waded through the new spring grass toward the castle site. The squeak of pulleys, the clink of chisels, and the deep clatter of stones sounded over the fields. Rye kept thinking he ought to tell Barley about wanting to go away on an adventure, but now that he knew Barley would want to go too it was even harder to know what to say.

Before the boys reached the castle site, they heard a cry from the direction of the village. "Sir Barley! Oh, Sir Barley! Help! Come quick!" Goody Butter ran toward them, holding her skirts hitched up. Her cap flew behind her, barely clinging round her neck by its ribbons.

"What's the matter?" Barley asked.

Goody Butter stopped, red-faced and gasping, and said, "Oh, Sir Barley, you have to help us. There's something awful in the well. Some kind of demon. It nearly drowned poor Molly Baker!"

"Is she all right?" Rye asked.

"She's all right, but that thing is still in the well, and it won't let anyone come near without giving them a choking!" Goody Butter said.

Barley stood up straight, threw back his shoulders, and said, "Of course I'll come at once. Don't worry, Goody Butter. Whatever it is, I'm sure we'll be able to take care of it." He flashed Rye a grin.

Rye grinned back. Maybe they didn't have to go out looking for adventures. Maybe an adventure had come to them.

EPISODE TWO: THE NIX IN THE WELL

ONE

Barley ran toward the village with Rye close behind. This was the first time since Barley had come home as a Knight of the Land Far Away that there had been any real trouble. Excited that he finally had a chance to do something to protect his village, but scared that he might not actually be able to do it, Barley hurried past the houses until he reached the well.

A few villagers stood in a small clump. Molly Baker sat on the ground, coughing and sobbing. Mother Baker rubbed her back and spoke to her, soft and soothing. Barley had been told that a demon in the well had tried to drown Molly, but Molly's hair and clothes were perfectly dry. She couldn't have fallen in the well, but she was still coughing like she'd swallowed a bucketful of water.

"What happened?" Barley asked.

"Molly went to draw the water, and as soon as the bucket came up, the water jumped out and choked her," Tildy Weaver said.

The bucket lay on the ground beside the well with its thick rope twining in the grass like a fat snake. "The water?" Barley asked, taking a step closer to the bucket.

"It was no water. It was a demon," said one of the new children, the stonemason's son. "I saw it. It had long teeth and big, bulgy eyes like a fish!"

"Aye, it was a nix. A water demon," one of the castle workmen said.

"Where's the demon now?" Barley asked.

"It jumped back into the well," Tildy said.

Barley drew his sword. "Stand back, everyone."

All the villagers took a step away from the well, except for Rye.

"Be careful, Barley," Rye said.

Barley nodded and strode to the rim of the well. He thought of the stories Sir Pinsky had told him and tried to remember what a knight should do when facing a foe. He squared his shoulders and stuck out his chest, like the knights he'd seen at King Hugric's court, then pointed his sword at the water. "Demon, come forth!" Barley did his best to make his voice sound bold and strong. "I challenge you! I am Sir Barley Fields, protector of this village and this well, and I say . . ."

A splash answered him from deep in the well. The villagers gasped and huddled closer together. Barley held his sword tight with both hands to keep it from shaking. The sloshing water fell silent. Barley crept to the edge of the well and looked down. Nothing but the bright blue sky and the shadowy reflection of his face touched the still surface.

Rye's head of straight, dark hair appeared in the reflection next to Barley's yellow curls. The two of them gazed down into the well. "Let's try drawing a bucket of water," Rye said softly.

Barley nodded. "You let the bucket down. I'll be ready with the sword."

Rye held the rope with one hand and dropped the bucket into the well with the other. The bucket hit with its usual echoing plop, the same sound Barley had heard nearly every day of his life when he'd gone to fetch water from this very well. Rye hauled the bucket up slowly as Barley held his sword ready.

Everyone in the village held their breath as the wooden bucket scraped lightly against the stones. When the bucket reached the rim of the well, Rye took the handle and set the bucket on the grass. The water sloshed in the bucket, then lay still.

"Maybe you scared it off!" Jep Weaver said.

The villagers let out a cheer.

With a ripple and a rush, the water in the bucket shot upward. The villagers' cheers turned to gasps and screams. A man only a little taller than Barley stood in the bucket. He was thin, with big, round eyes like a fish, and long hair that rolled and foamed like a waterfall. His clear wavering body caught and reflected in shimmering, shifting colors the village huts, the fields, and the sky.

"Be gone from this well, demon!" Barley pointed his sword and tried very hard to sound brave.

The demon threw his head back and opened his mouth in a silent laugh, showing long, glassy teeth.

Barley swung his sword at the demon. The demon didn't flinch as the blade whistled through his middle. Barley's sword splashed out a spray of sparkling drops of water, but the demon didn't seem to mind. Barley tried again, this time making a strike that should have taken the demon's head off. The demon simply watched with an irritated look on his face as the sword slashed right through his neck and came out the other side, dripping wet. Barley's mouth dropped open in surprise.

With a hiss like rushing water, the demon leaped at Barley's face and plunged down Barley's open mouth. Barley staggered backward as the water filled his chest. He tried to cough, but the water wouldn't come up. Rye rushed to his side. Barley doubled over, trying to force the demon up out of his lungs, but he couldn't do it. In terrified confusion, Barley dropped his sword. He stumbled forward and caught himself with his hands against the cold, hard stones of the well. His need to take a breath swelled in his chest until he felt he would burst.

Then, just as quick as it had gone in, the water inside him leaped out his throat and dove into the well with a plop.

Barley coughed, gasped, and spat out a last mouthful of water. Down in the well, the demon grinned up at him, then disappeared beneath the water's surface.

"Barley! Are you all right?" Rye pulled him away from the rim of the well.

Barley shook his head. "I don't know how to fight it," he said between coughs. If it had wanted to, the demon could have killed him, and there would have been nothing anyone could have done to stop it. The water burned his chest and tickled his throat. Sick to his stomach, and feeling like a failure, he wrapped his arms around himself and stared down at his boots.

Rye stared at his own boots for a moment, then his dark eyes flashed with that spark that meant he'd just come up with one of his tricks. "Wait here, Barley. I think I've got something. Could I borrow one piece of gold?"

TWO

A few minutes later, Rye came back with a piece of gold and a length of thin, strong rope.

"What are you going to do, Rye?" Barley asked.

Rye only shook his head and put a finger to his lips. He crept to the well and looked down. Then he took off one of his boots and set it on the ground. "Hello!" Rye called down into the well. With the rope behind his back, he held out the gold coin between his fingers so it flashed in the sun. "Hello down there! Do you want this?"

The water gurgled. Rye took a startled step backward. A sound like a stream flowing over rocks came echoing up the well's sides. The demon's face peeked over the rim. His colorless eyes fixed hungrily on the gleaming gold.

Rye dropped the coin into his boot.

Raising himself higher above the rim with thin, watery arms, the demon narrowed his eyes at Rye, peered at the boot, and then at Rye again. Rye took another small step away from the well, holding the coil of rope behind him with both hands. He gave the water demon a little nod, as if to say he was welcome to take the coin.

Fast as water pouring from a bucket, the demon flowed in an arc from the rim of the well into Rye's boot. As the demon disappeared inside, Rye dove for the boot. He grabbed the top and wrapped the rope around and around to bind the boot shut. The boot jerked and jumped, bulged as big as a pumpkin, but Rye held on tight. Barley rushed in to help and pinned the boot down while Rye tied the rope off with a strong, sturdy knot. The villagers shouted and cheered.

"That waterproofing spell keeps water on the outside, so it ought to keep water on the inside too," Rye said, admiring the struggling boot as it flopped on the ground.

"That's brilliant!" Barley said. "Now what do we do with it?"

"Let it go in the river?" Rye asked.

The boot made a loud squirting sound and a thin stream of water spat out the top. The stream of water thickened and began to form in the shape of the demon.

"Look out!" Barley said.

"I didn't tie it tight enough!" Rye dove for his boot and clamped his hands around the top, as if trying to squeeze it shut.

The demon flowed out of the boot, all except for one watery hand that was stuck inside, probably with fingers clamped on the coin. Scowling, the demon jerked and strained, but he seemed to be caught, unable to pull his hand free. Rye held on as the demon took a step toward the well, dragging the boot and Rye along with it.

Barley grabbed Rye and held on with both arms tight around his waist. Tom Cobbler grabbed Barley, and Tildy Weaver grabbed Tom, and soon all the villagers were holding on to each other and pulling with all their might. With the whole village hauling and shouting, they began to drag the demon away from the well and toward the river.

The demon dug his clear, wet feet into the grass, but with one hand in the boot, and Rye and the entire village pulling on that boot, he slipped farther and farther away from the well. With a terrible fierce scowl on his face, the demon clamped a long-fingered hand over Rye's nose and mouth. Rye shook his head from side to side, as if trying to get the demon's watery hand off his face. Barley felt Rye shudder and struggle to breathe.

"Let go, Rye!" Barley shouted. "Let him have the boot!"

Rye wouldn't let go.

The villagers took up the shout, calling for Rye to drop the boot. For an awful minute the demon stood, pulling against the entire village, with one hand in the boot and the other hand choking Rye. The demon watched with cold glassy eyes as Rye's movements slowed and became weaker. Finally, the boot slipped from Rye's hands.

As soon as Rye let go of the boot, the whole village tumbled backward in a heap. With one swift leap and a loud splash, the demon plunged back into the well, taking the boot along.

Sprawled on the ground with Barley still hanging on to him, Rye dragged in a ragged, wheezing breath. He coughed for a long time. Barley helped him sit up and watched anxiously as Rye's face went from pale bluish-white to its normal color.

Rye moaned. "My boot!"

Another gurgle from the well, and the boot came whistling through the air to smack Rye in the back of the head. The rope shot up after it and came tumbling down over Rye's shoulder.

Rye coughed a few more times and rubbed the wet spot in his hair where the boot had landed. He said, "We might need to go ask the Good Wizard Thornberry for that favor he owes us."

THREE

A nasty nix in the well meant everyone had to walk all the way to the river to fetch their water. The well was covered over with boards, and a hasty fence was put up around it to remind everyone to stay away. For the rest of the day, children who had errands in the village went the long way around, through the fields behind the houses, rather than taking the road that ran by the well.

Early the next morning, Barley and Rye set out for Wizard's Keep. Barley didn't like leaving his castle unfinished, but the workmen assured him that they would keep building while he was gone. For the important task of journeying to Wizard's Keep to learn how to get the nix out of the well, the castle workmen loaned Barley and Rye two of their best horses. The whole village came out to send them off and gave them presents of fresh-baked bread, sausages, cheese, dried apples, and warm hats and scarves to wear. Janet Grover even gave Barley a blue pebble she had found in the river. Barley promised everyone he would return soon with a way to banish the nix. Then he and Rye rode south along the river road.

"It's our first adventure together," Barley told Rye as they passed the bend in the river that marked the farthest south either of them had gone before. White blossoms covered the blackberry bushes, promising fruit later in the season. "This is the first time it's been just the two of us. We've always had someone with us. The king's messenger, or Sir Pinsky."

"You went alone to rescue me from Lost Castle," Rye said.

"That's true, and you went by yourself to the dragon's palace," Barley said. "So we've each been all on our own before, but now we're all on our own together!"

FOUR

The two brothers followed the White River Road down a wide valley ringed with forest. The forest gradually closed in on either side until toward evening, when both the river and the road plunged south into the trees. At the edge of the forest, another road led west toward the Red Mountains, and there at the crossroads stood an inn.

Barley turned to look back over the way they had come. Half in the gold of the sunset, half in the blue shadow of the Red Mountains, the White River Valley stretched away behind him. "All of that, Rye. Did you see it? All that land we rode through today. That's what the king gave me to protect." The same fear and delight he had felt when he heard there was a nix in the well thrilled through him, only ten times more. These were his lands, and though they were nothing more than a wide, empty river-bottom valley surrounded by the Lost Forest, he would watch over them as well as he could.

"Do you think this inn is under your protection?" Rye asked as he dismounted by the gate. Past a large, fenced yard the building stood with its back surrounded by trees and the front out in the open. A waterwheel creaked on one side, bringing water from the river up to a wooden trough that led into the building near the largest chimney. Rooms of all shapes and sizes sprouted under the thatched roof, either side by side or stacked on top of each other. Some rooms had windows as tall as a castle gate. Other rooms were so tiny, they might have been birdhouses. Some had stone walls, some brick, some wood, and some were of ordinary mud plaster like the cottages of Humble Village. It looked as if someone had taken pieces from dozens of different buildings and stuck them all together.

"Maybe only the front end of the inn," Barley said. "The back end is in the forest."

The front door opened, and a boy wearing a white apron and carrying a goose wing stepped out. "Welcome to the Lost Forest Inn!" he called. "If you'll come with me, I'll show you to the stables."

At first Barley wondered why this boy had a goose wing with him. Then, when the boy used the long white feathers to flip up the gate latch, Barley realized the goose wing was growing right out of the boy's shoulder instead of a left arm.

"Thank you," Rye said, staring at the wing too.

"If you're wanting to know what happened to me, don't bother asking. I'll tell you." The boy sounded bored. He walked around the side of the inn as Barley and Rye followed with their horses. As the boy talked, he waved the wing, gesturing with it like a hand. "A witch turned me into a goose because I took too long to bring her supper. To break the curse, my sister had to go without speaking for seven months and a day. She almost made it, but not quite, and it left me with one wing." As he finished the story, he tucked his wing up against his side like a goose would do. "I'm Willem, by the way, and my father's the innkeeper, and if there's anything we can do to make you more comfortable while you're here with us, please let us know."

"Can you tell us the best way to get to Wizard's Keep?" Barley asked.

"The shortest way is the road along the river. That road, if you can stay on it, eventually leads to Frog Pond. Once you cross the pond, the wizards live on the far side. But not many want to venture through the Lost Forest. If you take the road toward the Red Mountains, you can go around the forest and pass south of the pond, and then you'll find yourself at Wizard's Keep just the same."

"Oh, we don't mind going through Lost Forest," Barley said. "We've been in the forest lots of times."

"Suit yourselves," Willem said.

At the back of the inn, a pile of stones formed a huge cave with a little flickering fire inside. Barley looked closer and saw that the fire came from the open mouth of a small dragon that snored beside a gigantic sleeping black bear. Barley was glad those two were in the forest, so he wasn't responsible for making sure they were peaceable. They might have been angry with him if he woke them up in order to find out.

After feeding and caring for their horses, Barley and Rye followed Willem to the front door of the Lost Forest Inn.

Willem let them into a large room with far more tables and chairs than there were guests. A warm fire lit up a fireplace big enough for Barley to stand in. The burning logs hissed and sputtered as grease from a large roast dripped down on them, and the smell of meat and baking bread filled the room. Beside the fireplace, a canvas sack big enough that Barley could have curled up inside it hung from a fat iron spike in the wall. Barley wanted to ask Willem what the sack was for, but the boy had already crossed the room and was busy sweeping crumbs off an empty table with his goose wing.

At a table next to the fire sat two figures that Barley would have taken for ugly, oversized stone statues of a man and a woman if they hadn't both turned their heads to see who had come in. The firelight reflected sharply off their speckled gray skin, as if they'd been carved from solid rock. Trolls! Barley had heard of trolls, but these were the first he'd ever seen. At the far back of the room where the ceiling was higher, a gigantic man sat on the floor with his head in the rafters, drinking from a large wooden barrel. A giant! Barley hadn't expected to walk into an inn full of all the creatures the king's letter had ordered him to guard his lands against.

The smiling innkeeper, who was wearing a white apron like Willem's, called out from where he'd been ladling sauce over the roast. "Good evening, honored guests! Who are you, where do you come from, and where are you bound?"

"I am Sir Barley Fields of Humble Village," Barley said as boldly as he could. He scanned the whole room as he continued. "Protector of the White River Valley from

Humble Village to the edge of the Lost Forest. So if any of you are going to be unpeaceable, you'll have to do it at the forest end of the room, for if you come up here, I'm afraid I'll have to quell you!"

Rye looked as if he might like to shrink to nothing and disappear. Barley wondered if maybe he'd said something wrong.

The innkeeper laughed. "Thank you, Sir Barley. I'll let you know if I need any quelling done. Take a seat anywhere you like, and supper will be ready soon."

The trolls turned back to their conversation, and the giant showed no sign he'd heard Barley's speech at all. Barley watched them for another moment just to make sure they weren't going to cause any trouble, then followed Rye into the room.

They passed a raven, a fat white swan, and an oversized toad that sat around a table with a dish of live snails set at the center. "Your curse is looking much better this evening, Henrik," the swan said to the toad.

"Yes, thank you. I am feeling a little more like myself." Henrik the Toad croaked and snatched a snail into his mouth with his tongue.

At the next table sat the only other ordinary human in the room, a young man weeping over a bright orange flower in a large flowerpot. Barley had never seen such a flower, with so many petals and a ring of little yellow stars around its deep-red center. "Hello," Barley said to the weeping young man. "Are you all right?"

"Yes." The young man sniffled. His fine red jacket with its black trim and gold buttons, and the way his hazelnut-brown hair had been neatly tied back with a short black ribbon, reminded Barley of the nobles he'd seen at King Hugric's court. The young man's face would have been noble too if his nose and eyes hadn't been red from crying. "I'm all right. Sadly, I can't say the same for my true love. She's been like this for more than a year now." He gazed at the flower and sighed.

"Like what?" Barley asked.

"Like this!" The young man gestured impatiently at the flower. "This is Princess Zinnia. She's under a curse. I do hope I can find some way to break it by the wedding. We are to be married on Midsummer's Eve."

"That flower is really a princess?" Barley asked.

The young man nodded.

"So then, are you a prince?"

"Yes, Don't you remember me? I am Prince Aster, ninth son of King Hugric of the Land Far Away. We were introduced on the day of your knighting, Sir Barley."

"Oh," Barley said. He had been introduced to so many people that day, he couldn't remember any of them. "Yes, of course."

"That's quite the curse, Your Highness." The swan shook his head at the flower.

"What have you tried so far?" cawed the raven.

"I wept over her for a year and a day, but there's been no change," Prince Aster said.

"Did you try kissing her?" the toad asked.

"Alas, only love's first kiss has the power to break a curse, and I'd already kissed her once or twice before the curse befell her."

The frog made an amused grunt in his throat.

"We were engaged to be married! Of course I'd already kissed her," Prince Aster said indignantly. "At any rate, I am on my way to Wizard's Keep to see if anything can be done for her there."

"That's where we're going, too!" Barley said. "Do you want to go with us?"

"We're taking the road through the forest," Rye said.

"Excellent," Prince Aster said. "I, too, prefer the more direct route, and I am delighted to accept the company of such a famed knight of the realm. We journey together on the morrow."

EPISODE THREE: LOST FOREST

ONE

Rye didn't much like traveling with Prince Aster. Not only was the prince constantly fussing over his flower, singing to it or crying on it, or singing to it *while* crying on it, but Rye was worried that if any brave deeds came up Prince Aster might insist on doing them. Rye didn't want to go home to Humble Village until he proved himself worthy of becoming a knight. That was going to be hard when there was already a prince around, a prince with a mighty battle horse, a bow and a set of arrows, a sword even finer than Barley's, and a big, fancy shield. Rye was sure that if anyone needed rescuing, or anything needed slaying, Prince Aster would jump in and do it before Rye had a chance.

As the three of them—or four of them, counting the flower that was Princess Zinnia—rode through the Lost Forest, Prince Aster gave Barley advice on what to do if he ever came to court. It sounded complicated, having a lot to do with what kind of clothes to wear and which spoon to pick up first when at supper. Rye could tell Barley wasn't too interested.

The road along the river narrowed to a track and then faded to no more than a grassy path. At first, the path stayed close to the river, but then it wandered off into the trees. Choked by weeds and occasionally blocked by a dead fallen log, it looked like it hadn't been traveled for a long time.

They came to a place where the trees grew so thick, the travelers couldn't go forward. Rye realized he couldn't remember when he'd last heard the river, and thought they ought to try to find their way back to it. They turned around and rode back the way they had come, but instead of finding the river, they came to another dead end in the path.

"I think we're lost," Rye said.

"I thought you knew the way," Prince Aster said indignantly as he hugged his flowerpot tighter to his chest.

"We thought you knew the way," Barley said. "Didn't you say you preferred the more direct route?"

"I said that because I wanted to get to Wizard's Keep quickly, not because I'd tried both routes and decided I liked this one best. I've never been there before."

"Well, neither have we," Barley said.

"If we go downhill, we should be able to find our way back to the river," Rye said. "It can't be too far."

Barley stood up in his stirrups and pointed into the forest. "Look! It's a deer! I wonder if it's *my* deer." A handsome young deer with a short pair of antlers watched them from near the top of a ridge. Last summer, Barley had rescued a baby deer that had been lost in Grayfallow Swamp, and the two of them had become friends.

"I don't know if your deer would be in this part of the forest," Rye said. "It's probably some other deer."

"Hello!" Barley shouted up to the deer. "Is that you?"

The deer flicked its ears. It turned and walked over the ridge, out of sight.

"Wait!" Barley called out to the deer. He urged his horse to the top of the ridge.

Rye and Prince Aster followed. When they reached the top, Barley had ridden down into a little valley with a tiny stream trickling along the bottom, but the deer was gone.

"I don't think it was him," Barley said sadly.

"But look," Rye said. "If we follow this stream, it should take us to the river."

They followed the stream as it wound through the trees, widening and growing until at last it did join a larger river. Not knowing whether it was the White River or another river in the forest, the travelers followed it upstream for the rest of the day and camped on its banks that night.

In the morning, Prince Aster couldn't find his hat.

"Sorry," Rye said. "We should have warned you. It's the talking squirrels. They like to steal hats. Especially hats with feathers on them."

"Talking squirrels?" Prince Aster said as if he wasn't sure he believed such a thing was real.

"Oh, yes," Rye said. "We met one last summer. Didn't we, Barley?"

"Yes. It helped us find the way to Lost Castle," Barley said. "But I don't remember it stealing anyone's hat."

Rye raised his eyebrows, trying to signal Barley to play along. He checked to make sure Prince Aster was looking the other way, then pointed up into the tree where the hat hung high on a branch.

"Oh!" Barley said. "There it is!"

"Quite so," Prince Aster said. "Thank you, Sir Barley."

Rye couldn't tell if Prince Aster suspected anything. He certainly didn't act like he did. Prince Aster simply bound a handkerchief around the sharp end of one of his arrows and shot at his hat a few times until he knocked it down. Barley kept giving Rye sour scolding looks as if he couldn't believe Rye had stolen a prince's hat and hung it up in a tree.

They hadn't gone far along the river before they saw a wooden platform with a little straw hut on it bobbing in the middle of the river. Two sturdy ropes, one on either side of the platform, stretched from one shore of the river to the other. The ropes ran through rings at each corner of the platform so it could move back and forth across the river, but wouldn't be pulled downstream by the current. As Barley, Rye, and Prince Aster rode closer, an old man came out of the hut. His threadbare hood, his long, tangled hair, and his tattered robes were all the same bleached gray as an old piece of driftwood.

"Hello!" Barley called. "Is this the White River?"

The man took a long pole and used his stick-thin arms to push the platform toward the shore. He didn't speak a word until the platform scraped against the river rocks in the shallows.

"This is the White River," the old man said in a weary voice. "Do you wish to cross?"

"We're on our way to Wizard's Keep," Barley said. "But we've lost the road."

"There is no road through this part of the forest," the old man said. "But there are two villages across the river and the people who live there may be able to show you the way to Wizard's Keep."

"Then let's cross," Rye said.

"Is there a fee? Or a riddle we must solve? Some task we must do first?" Prince Aster asked the old man.

"No," the old man said. "I am bound by a curse to carry any who wish to go across the river. My ferry is small, and your fine horses are large, so one at a time, please."

Prince Aster crossed first, chatting away at the old man about his true love's curse and how he was going to Wizard's Keep to try to break it. The old man said nothing, only stuck his pole in the river, leaned on the pole as the ferry crept along its ropes, then drew the pole out and placed it again.

Barley went second, and as he rode across, he told the old man about the nix and how it was Barley's job as a knight and the protector of Humble Village to banish it from the village well. Rye crossed the river last. On the ride, he asked the old man if there was any way he could help him. Although freeing an old ferryman from a curse might not be the sort of brave deed that would earn Rye his knighthood, it would be a start.

"I must go back and forth across the river, carrying any who wish to cross," the old man said. "I know no more than that. When you get to Wizard's Keep, will you ask the wizards for me? Ask them if there is any way to break this curse."

"Of course," Rye said. "Thank you for taking us across the river."

TWO

Barley, Rye, and Prince Aster rode away from the river in the direction the old ferryman told them to go. Soon, the smell of savory roasted meats, delicious pies, warm breads, and sweet fruits called to them from somewhere up ahead. Their noses tickled, and their stomachs reminded them how long it had been since breakfast.

The travelers followed the wonderful smells until they came to a clearing in the woods where a small village stood under the noonday sun. Through each open door, Rye could see a table spread with a plain white linen tablecloth and piled with a feast. Juicy hams, brown turkeys, golden buttery rolls, cheeses, sausages, sugared cakes, crisp pies, grapes, apples, pears, and oranges loaded every table. Rye would have thought that a happy celebration must be going on, but the people in the houses all seemed sad. They ate very little and talked even less.

Prince Aster rode up to one of the huts and dismounted. "Good day to you!" he called in through the open doorway. "What is the great celebration in your village today that you have such feasts on your tables?"

"No celebration," answered a sad old woman who sat at the table with two little children, one on either side of her. "This is how we eat every day."

"Every day?" Barley said. "How? Where does all of this food come from?"

"It's like this." The old woman took the edge of the tablecloth and began to fold it up over the feast. All of the food vanished as if it had never been there. Barley made a very disappointed-sounding gasp, and Rye wished he had asked for a little taste before it was all gone. Then the old woman unfolded the tablecloth, shook it in the air three times, and spread it over the table. The food reappeared, another feast like the one that had been there before.

Prince Aster asked, "Does everyone in your village have such a marvelous tablecloth?"

"Yes," the old woman answered.

"Then how can you all be so sad?" the prince asked. "Not even my father, King Hugric, has his table spread with such a feast every day."

By now, several of the villagers had come out of their huts and gathered around the travelers.

"Are you a king's son, then?" one of the men asked.

"Maybe you can help us!" another villager said.

Rye said, "I'd like to help," but no one seemed to hear him. They were all trying to talk to the prince.

"Yes, I am Prince Aster, son of King Hugric of the Land Far Away, and I will help you if I can. What is your trouble?"

"This is the village of Crystal Springs," said the old woman as she came to the doorway of her hut. "We once had a spring of the sweetest water. It used to flow from this meadow down to the river, but now the spring is all dried up. Come and we will show you."

At the center of the meadow lay a small, empty hollow in the ground. A dry streambed, overgrown with grass, wound away from the hollow toward the river. The villagers watched anxiously as Prince Aster knelt beside the hollow and turned over a dusty rock. "Truly, this is very sad," he said. "As a prince of the Land Far Away, I can command many things, but I can't command the water to come up again in this spring. I'm afraid I can't help you."

The villagers sighed sadly and nodded their heads in understanding.

"But we're on our way to Wizard's Keep to ask them for help with our problems," Rye said. "We could ask them what to do about your spring."

"Oh, would you? Please?" asked one of the village children.

THREE

The villagers of Crystal Springs invited Barley, Rye, and Prince Aster to join them for a meal. Since it was such a nice, sunny day, the villagers brought out their tables and held a picnic in the meadow. Rye thought it was the best food he had ever tasted, even better than the food he remembered at King Hugric's castle.

When everyone had eaten as much as their stomachs could hold, and the travelers had loaded their bags with more food for their journey, the villagers folded up their tablecloths and all the dishes vanished. Rye promised the villagers he would ask the wizards what to do about their dry spring and then rode with Barley and Prince Aster into the forest.

After traveling south for about a day along the path the villagers had shown them, Rye thought he heard a distant sound of high, sweet bells. It was hard to tell for certain because Prince Aster was singing to his flower, again. He had a nice voice, but he had been singing the same song over and over for a very long time. As he sang, Barley and Rye kept rolling their eyes at each other behind his back.

"Excuse me," Rye said. "I'm sorry, Your Highness, but could you stop a moment? I thought I heard something."

The prince stopped his singing, and the three travelers reined their horses to stand still. In the quiet came a bright tinkling, as if fairies with bells on their heels danced somewhere nearby.

"Dare we go and see what it is?" Prince Aster asked. "Such sounds in an enchanted wood may only be to lure unwary travelers to their deaths."

"We dare," Barley said. "You can stay here with your flowerpot if you like."

Prince Aster hesitated at first when Barley and Rye rode in the direction of the bell sounds, but then he came along after them. Soon the bell sounds blended with the contented bleating of sheep. As the sounds grew clearer, Rye saw a bright gleam of gold between the trees. He tried to understand what it was—perhaps a field of ripe grain, or golden wildflowers in the sun.

Near the edge of the trees, Rye reined his horse to a stop and stared in surprise. Not grain or flowers, but houses made entirely of gold clustered in the small, shallow valley. A flock of sheep drifted like lazy little clouds over the grass, each one with a golden bell around its neck. Three girls with golden shepherds' crooks followed the sheep, one with black hair, one with brown, and the third one with wild red curls. The girls wore golden shoes, golden belts, delicate gold necklace chains around their necks, and had golden combs in their hair.

"The people who live here must be very rich," Barley said in amazement.

"Yes, but look," Rye said. "They're as sad as the people in the last village."

It was true. The three shepherdesses dragged their golden shoes through the grass and their sorrowful faces were turned down.

"Good morning, beautiful maidens," Prince Aster said. "What is the name of this place?"

"This is the village of Appledale," said the black-haired shepherdess. Her voice caught on the word "Appledale" as if she were near to tears.

"How is it that you can be so sad when surrounded by such wealth?" Prince Aster asked.

"The gold?" asked the brown-haired shepherdess. "That's nothing. We get that from the sheep."

"From the sheep?" Barley asked. "How?"

"Like this!" The red-headed shepherdess stuck her fingers in the woolly coat of the nearest sheep. "*Ring tickle rit rickle!*" She ruffled the sheep's coat. Gold coins dropped out of the sheep's wool and pinged down on the ground.

"Can I try?" Barley asked.

"Be my guest," the red-haired shepherdess said.

Barley climbed down from his horse and stepped up to a sheep, moving slowly and carefully so as not to startle it. He stuck his fingers in the sheep's wool and said, "Rinkle tinkle!" No matter how he ruffled, rubbed, and raked, nothing happened.

"It's *ring tickle rit rickle*," the black-haired shepherdess said.

"*Ring tickle rit rickle*," Barley said and rubbed some more. Coins spilled from the sheep's wool. Barley laughed and picked up a coin. "I'd have my castle built in no time if I had one of these sheep."

"You could build it out of solid gold," Prince Aster said.

"Gold and white river stone. Wouldn't that look nice?" Barley grinned.

"But what's troubling you?" Rye asked the shepherdesses, hoping they had a brave deed that needed doing. "Why are you so sad?"

"Our village used to have the most beautiful apple tree," the brown-haired shepherdess said. "It grew the sweetest apples in all the Emerald Realms. But this year, our tree hasn't grown a single leaf or blossom. We're afraid it's dead, but no one has the heart to cut it down. You can see it there in the village."

Rising over the tops of the golden houses, the bare branches of the old tree stretched like withered fingers to the sky. All the trees of the Lost Forest that ringed the valley were green with spring, but the tree at the center of the village seemed locked in winter.

"We're going to Wizard's Keep to ask the wizards what to do about a nix in our well," Rye said. "We could ask them what to do about your tree."

"That would be very kind of you," the black-haired shepherdess said.

"Do you know the way to Wizard's Keep?" Barley asked. He held out the coin to the brown-haired shepherdess, but she waved it away with a pout.

"South through the forest," the brown-haired shepherdess said. "There's a path that takes you to Frog Pond, and the keep is just beyond it. But no one in our village dares go that way. We dare not leave the village at all. There's a parataxis in the forest."

"That's dreadful!" Barley put the coin in his pocket. "I only have to pay one tax, and that's trouble enough. I would hate to have a pair of taxes. But if you have all this gold . . ."

"Not a pair of taxes!" the red-headed shepherdess said. "Parataxis!"

"Oh," Barley said. "What's that?"

"It's a terrible beast," said the black-haired shepherdess. "Long like a giant snake, with over a hundred legs, and each section of its body is made from some poor creature it has swallowed."

"If it finds you, you'll all be eaten," the red-headed shepherdess warned.

Slaying a monster like that sounded like a brave deed that needed doing, but Rye wasn't as excited about it as he thought he would be. He'd been hoping to start out with something more ordinary, like a princess who had to be rescued from a giant or a troll that needed to be driven out from under a bridge. Barley gave Rye the same wide-eyed, frightened look that he had last summer when Rye told him that it was a knight's job to slay dragons and things.

"We have no fear of such a monster," Prince Aster said. "I am Prince Aster of the Land Far Away, and this is Sir Barley Fields, and if we should meet such a beast, I am sure we can slay it."

Barley swallowed hard, put on a forced smile, and nodded.

FOUR

Prince Aster had said he had no fear of the parataxis, but as they rode away from Appledale and into the forest, he wasn't singing anymore.

Rye asked Barley, "If we see this parataxis, do you think I could borrow your sword so I could try to slay it?"

"Absolutely not!" Prince Aster cut in before Barley could answer. "If we should see this parataxis, you will both stay back while I confront the beast. Your prince commands it."

"Your Highness?" Rye asked. "I want to do some brave deed so I can be knighted like my brother. If you let me slay the parataxis, do you think that would be brave enough?"

"Slay the parataxis so you can be made a knight?" Prince Aster asked, surprised. "I'm afraid you don't understand how these things work. A knight must be from a noble family and spend years in training as a squire, and then do *many* brave deeds before knighthood is bestowed."

"But Barley was made a knight for driving the brigands out of Lost Castle," Rye said.

"Ah, that. Yes." Prince Aster frowned. "That was something of an exception. You see, my father desperately needed someone to slay the Dragon of the Deep. He hoped that whoever had been strong enough to single-handedly defeat the Lord of Lost Castle and his band of brigands would also be able to slay a mighty sea dragon. That is why your brother was summoned to the castle and granted knighthood. The kingdom was in great need, and so an exception was made. It is not the way it usually happens."

Rye's heart felt as empty as looking in the cellar and finding that there's nothing left to eat. He had imagined that all he had to do was one brave deed, and then he could be knighted. If what Prince Aster said was true, Rye would have to do so much more. Years of training? A squire?

"You could be my squire," Barley offered.

Rye didn't say anything. He didn't like the idea of being Barley's squire, but maybe he could ask Sir Pinsky. Yes, once the nix was out of the well, Rye would go and find Sir Pinsky and offer him his services as a squire. Sir Pinsky had said that Barley and Rye had been the finest adventuring companions he'd ever had. Rye was sure Sir Pinsky would be glad to take him.

Or maybe Prince Aster was wrong. Maybe Rye didn't have to become a knight in the usual way. If there had been an exception for Barley, maybe there could be an exception for Rye.

Episode Four: Wizard's Keep

ONE

The travelers saw no sign of the parataxis either that day or the next. On the third day after they had passed through Appledale, Prince Aster said perhaps the parataxis was only an imaginary creature the villagers had invented to frighten their children and keep them from wandering off into the forest. Barley hoped the prince was right, but Rye seemed a little disappointed that there wouldn't be a terrible monster to fight on their way to Wizard's Keep.

Barley wished he was more like Rye, who never seemed to be afraid of anything. If the parataxis did show up, Barley wondered if he ought to loan Rye his sword. No, Barley was the knight, and it was his job to help the prince slay the monster. What Rye really needed was a nice sword of his own, especially if Rye was going to be Barley's squire. Barley thought about buying a sword for Rye with some of the gold King Hugric had given him. Then he remembered the castle, and the taxes, and wasn't sure if he'd have enough left over for a nice sword for his brother.

Late one afternoon, they came to the shore of a wide lake. In the water stood two rows of weathered posts as if there had been a dock once, but it had long ago fallen apart. They couldn't see the shore to the east or the west, and only the faintest green traces of low hills rose above the water far to the south.

"No going south now," Barley said. "Unless anyone's brought a boat."

"What is this lake?" Prince Aster asked. "I don't recall anyone mentioning a lake."

"There was supposed to be a pond," Rye said. "But we've been away from the road for so long, we might have missed it."

"Do you think we've missed Wizard's Keep?" Barley asked.

"We shall have to inquire of the first persons we encounter," the prince said.

The travelers made camp for the night. In the morning, they worked their way along the lakeshore. As the sun rose higher, sailboats began to dot the water, but these boats were too far away for the travelers to call out to and ask directions.

About midmorning, they came to a town at the edge of the lake. The town had a high wall around it, with gates that faced the docks. Some fishermen sorted their catch while others prepared their boats to sail out for the day.

"Good morning!" Prince Aster called to a crew of fishermen who were climbing into their boat. "What place is this?"

"This is the town of Frogshead, on Frog Pond," the oldest fisherman said.

"Frog Pond?" Barley looked around for a pond, but he couldn't see one anywhere. "Where is it?"

The fishermen laughed.

"You can't miss it. It's right there," said the youngest fisherman, who looked only a little older than Rye. He pointed to the vast lake behind him.

"That's a pond?" Barley asked. He'd been expecting that when they came to Frog Pond, it would be a little puddle, not a huge lake.

At least this meant they hadn't been lost. They were on the right track, and Wizard's Keep would be just on the other side of the water.

Prince Aster said, "We need to get across. We have important business with the wizards at Wizard's Keep. Will you give us passage?"

TWO

Prince Aster paid the fishermen for the use of their boat. The oldest fisherman, who was the father of the rest of them, sent all his sons home except for the youngest, who came along to help with the sailing. Barley, Rye, and Prince Aster led their horses down the dock and onto the fishing boat. Barley hadn't been on a boat before, and he liked the creak of the wood and the way the sails filled with wind and drew them across the water. Rye wanted to know everything about how the boat worked. He stayed close to the fisherman's son, asking questions and trying for himself everything the fisherman's son would let him do. Prince Aster stood at the front of the boat, holding his flower close and watching the distant shore.

As the sun rose higher, the shore behind them became no more than a thin line of green trees between the bright blue sky and the deep blue lake. The Red Mountains rose up in the distance, coming out of the forest like islands out of a sea. Barley thought of his half-built castle of river stone that stood beside the White River, far away and out of sight beyond the trees, along with his village, his parents, his friends, and the well that needed to be freed of an unwelcome nix. He missed all of it and wished he were on his way home already, but if he was going to do his duty to protect his village, he knew he had to go on.

When the sun had passed overhead, Barley could make out another walled town on the far side of the lake. The fisherman and his son pointed their boat toward it. "Frogsfoot," the fisherman said. "Nearest town to Wizard's Keep. They do good trade on potions and amulets made by the wizards. Ship them to all the towns around the lake. They keep their market stocked with things the wizards need for their spells, too."

"Where is the Keep?" Prince Aster asked.

"It's a bit of a ride back into the hills," the old fisherman said. "There's a good wagon road between Wizard's Keep and the town. You shouldn't have any trouble."

THREE

The fishermen tied their boat up to a dock by Frogsfoot. They told Prince Aster that they had a few errands of their own in town and would be ready to take everyone back across the lake the next day. Eager to reach Wizard's Keep before sundown, Barley, Rye, and Prince Aster rode quickly through Frogsfoot Market. Barley wished they could have stayed longer to look at the market stalls. Gleaming bottles of colored potions, bins of polished stones, racks of charms and amulets, and even a few displays of swords lined the street. Barley noticed Rye turning his head to stare at the swords and decided that he simply had to find a way to get his brother a sword of his own.

After taking the south gate out of Frogsfoot, they followed the road through the hills until they came to the strangest castle Barley had ever seen. Not that he'd seen that many castles. Only two, both of them last summer. Lost Castle had been four towers connected by a single sturdy outer wall that surrounded an open courtyard. King Hugric's castle had been an immense building with domes, balconies, gables, and many towers reaching gracefully to the sky. This castle, Wizard's Keep, had only one tower, fat and round, with windows placed at random, as if it were a tall cake that some small child had naughtily poked a finger into wherever they wanted. The top level had no roof—only a railing that caged in a collection of strange metal objects with parts that whirled or twisted in the wind. Surrounding the tower at some distance, stone walls thick enough to have rooms inside them enclosed a large square courtyard. A wide walkway ran along the top of the walls, and a two-story gatehouse with a thatched roof faced the road.

As they rode up to the gatehouse, they passed a fenced garden. A row of turnips with round purple tops the size of washtubs grew beside beanstalks with flowers as black as crow feathers and a single bush with at least a dozen different kinds of berries growing on it. Several large, colorful birds with long necks and tails nested high on top of the roof of the gatehouse. When he got close, Barley could see they weren't birds. They were tiny bat-winged dragons!

"Look, Rye!" Barley pointed to the roof. "There's some dragons for you. Those don't look like they'd be hard to fight!"

Rye laughed. Barley hadn't seen Rye looking this happy in a long time. Rye slowly turned his head, taking in the outer wall of Wizard's Keep. Then he stared up at the top of the tower as if he'd like nothing better than to be up there himself.

Prince Aster reined his horse to a stop in front of the gatehouse's open double doors. "Sir Barley, as a knight of the

Land Far Away, it will be your duty to announce me at the gate," he said.

Nervous, but grinning, Barley asked, "What do I say?"

"Tell them who we are and what we want," Prince Aster said.

Barley shouted, "Announcing Prince Aster of the Land Far Away! I am Sir Barley Fields of Humble Village, and this is my brother, Rye! We would like to see the Wizard Thornberry, please!"

Prince Aster frowned, cleared his throat, and pointed at the flowerpot tucked in the crook of his elbow.

"And also presenting the Princess Zinnia!" Barley added.

Prince Aster gave him a smile and a nod.

Three heads poked out of an upstairs window of the gatehouse, two boys and a girl in short, pointed hats, each one a different color. "You're not really!" said the one in the brown hat, the youngest, a boy about Barley's age.

"Yes," the prince said. "I am indeed Prince Aster, and this is the Princess Zinnia." He hefted the flowerpot a little higher so the boy could see.

"No, no, I mean your friends there. Are you really Sir Barley and Rye Fields?"

"Yes," Barley said, confused that these young wizards seemed more excited to see him than to see a prince at their gate.

The girl in the red hat gasped, then squealed, "Wizard Thornberry told us all about you!"

"Come in!" the older boy said. He wore a blue hat with a slightly taller peak than the other two.

"I'll go and fetch Wizard Thornberry," the younger boy said.

The three heads disappeared from the window, and a clatter of footsteps sounded inside the gatehouse. As Barley led his horse through the gate and under the archway, he saw the younger boy pelting across the courtyard, holding his short, pointed hat hard on his head while his brown robes flapped around his legs. A black-footed ferret bounded in bouncy little arcs beside him. The girl in red met Barley on the far side of the arch, adjusting her own hat and smiling. She kept opening her mouth as if she wanted to say something, but then she would blush and look away. The bright-eyed field mouse on her hat brim blinked at Barley and raised its nose to sniff the air, showing its delicate yellow teeth. The older boy bowed to Prince Aster and offered to take their horses to the stables. As the older boy led the three horses away, Barley noticed the bright green head of a snake peeking out of the hood that hung down the back of the boy's blue robes.

Most of the wizards in the courtyard stopped what they were doing to come over and greet the newcomers. They all bowed or curtsied respectfully to the prince, but it was Barley and Rye they were most interested in. By the time the younger boy from the gatehouse came back, bringing both Wizard Thornberry and a short girl in black braids and spectacles, Rye was answering all sorts of questions about the selkie boy he'd met last summer, and Barley was telling another group of wizards about the magic sword he'd used to fight the Lord of Lost Castle.

"Excuse me!" the prince said, plainly irritated. "Could I please get some assistance?"

"Yes, of course," Wizard Thornberry said. "Welcome to Wizard's Keep. Welcome, all of you." He took off his dark purple hat and made a low bow. The magpie on his shoulder dipped its head as well, and the spectacled girl at Wizard Thornberry's side gathered up her own dark purple robes and bobbed a polite curtsy. As Wizard Thornberry straightened, he said, "Sir Barley, I see you've brought a troubled prince to consult with me."

"Yes, if you don't mind," Barley said. "And we have some troubles of our own that we'd like to ask you about."

Wizard Thornberry nodded and said, "Come with me to my study. We'll see what we can do."

FOUR

As Barley, Rye, and Prince Aster followed him across the courtyard, Wizard Thornberry nodded to the girl who walked at his side and said, "Allow me to introduce you to Briar, my granddaughter."

"And your apprentice!" Briar said indignantly.

"And my apprentice." Wizard Thornberry smiled at her fondly.

"Very nice to meet you, Apprentice Briar," Prince Aster said. "Thank you for welcoming us to Wizard's Keep."

Briar stopped to curtsy again, then ran to catch up with her grandfather.

They all followed Wizard Thornberry around the large tower at the center of the courtyard to a small building that snuggled into the corner of the courtyard wall. Smoke rose from a messy tangle of thatch on the roof.

"Cursed pygmy dragons!" Wizard Thornberry muttered. He took a wand from his pocket and pointed it at a bucket of water beside the doorstep. Barley gasped as the bucket rose high into the air, hovered over the smoldering spot, and dumped its water. A surprised miniature dragon let out an angry squawk and glared down at Wizard Thornberry. It shook out a pair of wet wings with a snap and then settled out of sight in its nest.

The bucket dropped into its spot by the doorstep with a satisfied clatter. Barley clapped his hands.

"Did you like that spell?" Wizard Thornberry asked as he pressed down the latch and swung the door open. "It took me quite a while to set it up. The bucket will automatically refill itself with water in a few minutes. It's always ready when I need it to douse the roof."

"I've used it to put out a few fires inside the workshop, too," Briar said proudly.

"That you have," Wizard Thornberry said. "Please come in, everyone."

Inside Wizard Thornberry's workshop, shelves and sets of tiny drawers lined every inch of the walls. Books and scrolls, bottles and jars, skulls and bones, and gleaming metal tools with hinged parts and strange markings packed the shelves and spilled out in piles on the floor. Wizard Thornberry's magpie fluttered to perch on a coil of glass tubing.

At first, Barley wondered how the workroom could look four times as large on the inside than it had looked on the outside. Then he realized that most of the room was inside the courtyard wall and underneath the walkway, like the arch under the gatehouse had been. A window in the side wall showed a fine view of the road and a little bit of Frog Pond in the distance.

Briar yanked an old wooden stool from one pile of clutter and set it down next to Rye. Next, she moved an armload of scrolls out of a high-backed cushioned armchair and motioned for the prince to take a seat. As Barley tried to help her free a wicker chair from what looked like the skeleton of a giant snake, he accidentally knocked over a tower of books with his elbow. The books pelted down onto the rug with dusty thumps.

"I'm so sorry," Barley said, and bent to pick up a book. Rye knelt down to help him.

"Don't worry about it. The brownies will take care of it," Briar said. When Barley picked up a second book, she said, annoyed, "No, honestly, you don't know what order those books were in. Leave it for the brownies."

"Order?" Barley looked around the room. Nothing seemed to be in any kind of order at all.

Briar glared at him through her spectacles. "Every single thing in this room is exactly where my grandfather wants it to be, and he knows exactly where to find everything. It's in perfectly good order."

Rye gasped at an open book in front of him on the floor. "I know some of these words!" he said, pointing to the page. Then his face turned red. He glanced self-consciously at Wizard Thornberry.

"Have you been learning to read?" Wizard Thornberry asked.

"Not really," Rye said as he stood up, keeping his eyes on the book. "I used the king's letter and Barley's pictures that he drew when you read it. I know all the words in the letter now, and I can write them out from memory, but that's all I know how to do."

Wizard Thornberry beamed. "I'm impressed. Very impressed. I'd like to have a talk with you later, Rye, but first let's see what we can do to help Prince Aster."

FIVE

Prince Aster set his flowerpot on Wizard Thornberry's worktable and then sank down in the cushioned chair. "This is my true love, the Princess Zinnia," the prince said with a sorrowful nod toward the flower.

"Ah!" Wizard Thornberry's bushy gray eyebrows jerked up so fast that they knocked his hat back. He caught his hat before it toppled, straightened it, and said. "Yes, you definitely have a problem. Please tell me everything you know."

While the prince told the very long story of his courtship with the Princess Zinnia, Wizard Thornberry gathered bottles and jars from around the room and set them on the table. Barley sat in the wicker chair by the window and wished Prince Aster would hurry up and get to the important part of the story. The prince wasn't the only person here who needed advice. As Barley's gaze wandered around the room, he noticed that the pile of books he had knocked over had begun to stack themselves up. The books never moved when Barley was looking at them, but if he turned his head and watched Wizard Thornberry pour liquids into the little cauldron on his worktable, when Barley glanced back at the pile, another book would be on the stack.

"And then the next morning, when her serving maid went to wake her for the day, she found only this flower in her bed, with its blossom on the pillow." Prince Aster brushed a tear from his eye and then shook the tear off his finger and into the flowerpot. "She had been cursed to become this flower. Our wizard at the castle suggested that I weep over her for a year and a day. I have done so faithfully, but she hasn't transformed."

"Briar, would you bring me an empty vial please?" Wizard Thornberry asked. Briar hopped up from the workbench where she'd been sitting beside her grandfather, went to one of the shelves, and came back with a small clear glass bottle. Wizard Thornberry dipped a ladle into his cauldron and then poured the liquid carefully into the vial. "Now close the windows," he said.

Already at the front window, Briar snapped the shutters closed. When all the windows in the room were shut with only the tiniest streaks of sunset gold peeking through, the Wizard Thornberry held the vial close to the flower's blossom. After a moment, he pulled the vial away from the flower, shook it, and then held it close again. He made a short grunt of surprise in his throat.

"What?" Prince Aster asked. "What is it?"

"This is not the Princess Zinnia," Wizard Thornberry said. "This was an ordinary flower."

Episode Five: The Council of Wizards

ONE

"What did you say?" Prince Aster asked in a weak, shaky voice.

"This can't be your true love." Wizard Thornberry gestured to the flower. "It's not a princess, and it never was one. No one saw your princess actually transform into this flower, did they?"

"No." The prince seemed to be having trouble catching his breath.

"I would carefully question the princess's serving maid, then. Your princess may have transformed into something else, or perhaps, sad to say, she merely left the flower as a parting gift and ran off. Was this an arranged marriage?"

"This flower is not Princess Zinnia? How do you know this to be true?" Prince Aster demanded.

"Briar, would you please bring me that cursed imp skull, the one in the chest behind the keg of silverfish paste?"

After tying on a leather apron and shoving her hands down a pair of heavy gloves, Briar disappeared into the shadows of the darkened workroom. She came back with a small iron chest in her arms. The moment she lifted the lid, the vial in Wizard Thornberry's hand glowed bright red. The light reflected off Briar's spectacles and bathed a horned skull resting on a pillow inside the chest.

Wizard Thornberry said, "This vial contains a potion that indicates the strength and nature of a curse by the light it gives off in the curse's presence. As you've already seen for yourself, the vial does not react when near this flower. Therefore, this flower has no curse on it. On the other hand, the curse on this skull . . ." Wizard Thornberry shuddered. "Thank you, Briar, You may put that away now."

The light from the vial winked out as the lid of the chest snapped shut. Barley realized he'd been holding his breath and pressing himself far back in his wicker chair. On the other hand, Rye leaned forward, curious, eager, his eyes full of unasked questions.

Prince Aster jumped out of his chair. "I must go and learn what has become of my true love!" He dashed to the door and tore it open. At the sudden movement, the magpie woke up and let out a surprised croak.

"One moment, Your Highness," Wizard Thornberry said, but Prince Aster had run out into the courtyard, leaving the door swinging open behind him.

"My horse!" Prince Aster shouted. "Bring me my horse at once!"

Wizard Thornberry sighed and rubbed his forehead with his thin fingers. "Briar, would you please go and tell His Highness the prince that there's something important he should know before he gallops off to find his true love?"

From out in the courtyard came the sound of Prince Aster jumping into his saddle and galloping through the front gate.

"He's already gone," Briar said.

"Go fetch him back," Wizard Thornberry said.

"But Poppy!" Briar protested.

"Hurry now, or you might not catch him."

Briar grumbled angrily, "Promise you won't do anything *interesting* until I come back!" She threw her gloves and apron on the floor, then ran through the doorway.

Barley opened the window shutter to see Prince Aster on his big black warhorse gallop away down the road until he passed out of sight behind the first line of hills. A moment later, a small girl in a short, pointed hat with her braids and purple robes streaming behind her went riding by on the back of a . . . what was that? A hairy yellow beast as big as a bear, but as lean as a wolf. It had huge paws, a face like a cat, and a bush of thick brown fur around its head. Barley had never seen anything like it. It tore along the road as fast as Prince Aster's horse had run and was out of sight by the time Barley thought to ask the wizard what it was.

Barley drew a quick gasp and whirled around. "Rye? You didn't switch flowers on Prince Aster, did you?"

"No! Of course not!" Rye said, so honestly surprised that Barley felt he must be telling the truth. "Where would I have gotten a flower like that?"

"Found it growing in the woods," Barley said. "I don't know." He still couldn't believe Rye had found some piece of paper that looked like the letter from King Hugric and switched the two so that Barley had carried the paper around for weeks without noticing.

"Well, while we wait for them to come back . . ." Wizard Thornberry scratched his head beneath his hat as his magpie fluttered over to settle on his shoulder. "Sir Barley, what can I do for you?"

Two

Rye listened as Barley told Wizard Thornberry about the nix in their well. The wizard nodded and made little grunting sounds in his throat as he walked around and opened the windows. The sun had nearly set, and so the light in the workshop stayed dim. Rye wondered at all the books piled around him, wishing he could read them to see what secrets they held. He wanted to know what every bottle, jar, and tool in the room was for. Wizard Thornberry lit a few candles, and the glass and metal objects on the shelves sparkled brighter than a bag of gold. Rye didn't understand it, but he felt as comfortable and content in this workroom as he did sitting on his mother's hearth at home.

"A nix in the well is a tricky thing indeed," Wizard Thornberry said as he settled himself in the high-backed cushioned chair Prince Aster had been using. The magpie stuck its head in the top pocket of Wizard Thornberry's robes and came out with a fat dried beetle, which it snapped up with two clicks of its beak. "I know how to recover a youth or a maiden who has been taken by a nix, and how to win your voice back if a nix steals it from you, but I don't know how to remove a nix from a well. No one has drunk any water from the well since the nix was in it, I hope?"

"No," said Barley. "I don't think so. We boarded it up and put a fence around it."

"Good, very good. I'm sorry, but I simply can't recall a single case in which a nix has been removed from a well. I'll have to consult with the council. It may take a few weeks of study and research to uncover an answer for you, if there is one at all."

"Weeks?" Barley cried out in dismay. "We need our well back now!"

Rye felt a little bit guilty at how happy it made him to think of spending weeks at Wizard's Keep. He knew that everyone at home would be anxious to have their well again. Still, he hoped it took Wizard Thornberry a good long time to find a solution to their problem, and that they could stay until he did.

"Or you could do it the easy way," Wizard Thornberry said.

"What's that?" Barley asked.

"Dig a new well."

"A new well?" Barley asked.

"Yes, a good quarter mile from the first one so the nix isn't likely to have some underground stream it can take to get between them."

"A quarter mile?" Barley protested. "The river's not a quarter mile from the village. We might as well keep hauling our water from there."

"As I said, I will ask the council for you," Wizard Thornberry said. "But I do think it may be best to dig another well."

Barley sagged in his chair, clearly disappointed.

"Wizard Thornberry?" Rye asked.

"Yes?"

"As we came through Lost Forest, we met some other people who needed help. The first was an old man who was cursed so he has to ferry people across the river. Then there was a village where every house has a magic tablecloth that makes a feast whenever you shake it three times and spread it over a table, but the people are sad because their spring has gone dry. And there was a village where the sheep drop gold coins out of their wool, but the people are sad because their apple tree hasn't budded or bloomed at all this spring. I promised each of them we would ask at Wizard's Keep if there's anything that can be done."

Wizard Thornberry listened to Rye with a very serious look that grew darker with each story. "The council will want to hear of this," Wizard Thornberry said. "I'll arrange for them to meet with you as soon as possible. First thing in the morning."

THREE

Barley and Rye followed Wizard Thornberry and his magpie to the dining hall, a long building that ran half the length of the southern courtyard wall. Wizards and apprentices in their colored robes sat at the tables, eating bowls of stew and rolls of plain brown bread. Rye hadn't expected that wizards would eat such ordinary food.

At one end of the room, a woman with an apron over her wizard robes and her hair wrapped in a scarf stood on a small ladder to ladle soup out of a cauldron as tall as Barley. Wizard Thornberry waited in line with Barley and Rye for their turn to be served.

When Barley picked up his spoon and his bowl of stew, the woman at the cauldron asked, "Do you want it glamoured?"

"What's that?" Barley asked.

"Glamoured. So you think you're eating whatever you want. It's turnip stew, but if you don't like that, I can glamour it for you."

"You mean, you can turn it into something else?" Barley asked.

"No. Glamour only makes you *think* you're eating something else. What'll it be? Tell me quick. You're holding up the line."

"Sausage pie, please!" Barley held out his bowl.

The woman took a big shaker and sprinkled sparkling powder over Barley's stew.

Barley gasped. "Look, Rye. It's sausage pie!"

It still looked like turnip stew to Rye. "I don't see it," Rye said. "Nothing happened."

"You try it," Barley said.

Rye held out his bowl and said, "Mushroom tarts, please." The woman sprinkled the sparkling powder over the top. As soon as the sparkles settled into the bowl, the steaming stew became a pile of flaky little open-faced tarts filled with chopped mushrooms and gravy.

"Ew, mushroom tarts!" Barley said.

"You don't have to think *you're* eating them," Rye said. He put his nose close to his bowl, enjoying the hearty, tingly smell of the hot mushrooms.

"I'm glad yours still looks like stew to me or I wouldn't want to sit by you," Barley said. "You could have anything you want, and you pick mushroom tarts?"

"Sir Barley! Rye! Come sit with us!" The younger boy from the gatehouse waved at them from a table halfway across the room. Wizard Thornberry nodded for them to go on, so Barley and Rye took their bowls and went to join the boy and the other apprentices at his table.

"Tell us all about the Dragon of the Deep," the boy asked eagerly as they sat down. As Barley described the dragon, making him even larger and scarier than he actually was, Rye reached into his bowl and picked up one of his mushroom tarts.

The apprentices at the table stared at Rye, looking shocked and disgusted.

"You realize you're eating your stew with your fingers," said a girl in pale blue robes with a black rabbit on her lap.

Rye paused with the mushroom tart about an inch from his open mouth. It looked like a mushroom tart to him, but when he checked everyone else's bowls, including Barley's, all they had was stew. Cold, uncomfortable embarrassment slithered into his stomach as he imagined them seeing a lump of boiled turnip dripping in his fingers.

"No matter what you think you're eating, you eat it with the spoon." The dark-skinned boy next to Rye patted him on the shoulder. A gray fox cub lay curled up and dozing on the bench between them.

"What do you think you're eating?" Rye asked the boy with the fox cub.

"Fish curry. At home I would eat it with my fingers, but here, a spoon is the polite way to do it."

Rye set the mushroom tart back in his bowl and looked around for some way to wipe off the invisible gravy he knew had to be on his fingers. A girl across the table with a colorful parrot on her shoulder handed him a cloth napkin.

"What are you having?" he asked her.

"Fresh cherries," she said. "Though I forgot to tell Cook to leave the pits out." She put a spoonful of stew in her mouth, chewed as if she were trying to avoid biting down too hard on a cherry pit, then made a face and swallowed.

Rye picked up his spoon and cut into one of the tarts. It was the best mushroom tart he had ever tasted.

The apprentice wizards listened eagerly as Barley and Rye told them of their encounter with the Dragon of the Deep. With all the questions the apprentices asked, the story lasted long after everyone had finished eating and most of the wizards had left the dining hall. Wizard Thornberry sat down at the next table and waited for them. He seemed to be enjoying the discussion too.

The dining hall door creaked open. Briar dragged herself in, head down, spectacles crooked, black braids ragged and windblown. Rye waited for Prince Aster to appear behind her, but he didn't.

"I'm sorry, Grandfather. He got away," Briar said. "I chased him all the way to the docks, but he got in a boat and sailed off before I could catch him. Who knew that big old warhorse could run so fast? And then Algernon was so tired, he had to walk all the way back."

"Algernon?" Wizard Thornberry asked, surprised. "You went after him on Algernon?"

"Of course I did," Briar said. "Why wouldn't I?"

"No wonder Prince Aster ran from you. The poor fellow probably thought a hungry lion was chasing him," Wizard Thornberry said.

"A lion!" Barley said. "So that's what it was. I saw you out the window and wondered what that was you were riding on."

"But . . . Algernon's an enchanted lion. He only eats cabbages," Briar said.

"Well, you wouldn't know it to look at him," Wizard Thornberry said.

FOUR

Late that night, too excited to sleep, Rye sat at the window in the small guest room near Wizard Thornberry's workshop, listening to Barley's soft, contented snores. Outside, strange animals in their pens called to one another, the pygmy dragons trilled in their nests, and the wind creaked the metal windmills and whirligigs on top of the tower. Tomorrow Rye would see the Council of Wizards. It thrilled and terrified him, even more than trying to escape from Lost Castle, or facing the Dragon of the Deep. He didn't understand why he felt both as if he wanted to run away, and as if he'd give anything to have this chance to meet the council tomorrow.

FIVE

The next morning, Barley and Rye waited in front of the door to the tower of Wizard's Keep for Wizard Thornberry to bring them up to see the council. Unlike the cut and carefully placed stones of the courtyard wall, the stones of the tower were piled together in all different sizes and shapes. Instead of an arch, a flat slab of stone stretched over the doorway. It made the tower seem much older than the rest of the Keep, part of an ancient world that had passed out of memory.

Rye's heart thumped harder as the door to the tower creaked open. Wizard Thornberry peeked out. "The council is ready for you," he said. "Come in."

Once inside, Rye drew in a long gasp when he saw that the stairs went down as well as up. "How far does it go down?" he asked.

"As far as it goes up," Wizard Thornberry said. "All things in balance."

The stairs wound around, following the wall of the tower. As they climbed, they passed one open door to a room packed with shelves of books and scrolls, and another to a room where wizards studied at long tables or worked over their cauldrons. Near the top of the stairs, a wizard carrying a tall mirror came out of a room. Before the wizard closed and locked the door behind him, Rye caught a glimpse of boots, cloaks, swords, shields, mirrors, chests, crowns, lamps, bottles, and hats—as jumbled together as the Dragon of the Deep's treasure piles had been.

Wizard Thornberry stopped on the last landing. The stairs reached up high into the shadows to a little trapdoor in the distant ceiling. Rye wanted to go up there and see what was on top of the tower, but he thought he would wait to ask until after they'd spoken to the council.

"The council will hear you now," said a woman with a sword buckled at her side. "Go in and take a seat."

Barley and Rye followed Wizard Thornberry through the double doors into a vast round room that must have taken up the entire top floor of the tower. High overhead, wooden beams and stone ledges faded into shadow as if there were no ceiling at all up there, only an endless dark that reached into the sky.

Shafts of sunlight from narrow windows lit seven chairs where seven wizards sat in a circle around the room. Most of them looked human, except for one wizard woman with a pair of golden wings behind her back and a sandy brown animal's paw peeking out beneath the bottom of her robes. Rye had to work hard to swallow down his terror until he saw the wizards' kind, wise smiles.

Barley plopped down in the middle of three empty chairs facing the council. Wizard Thornberry nodded respectfully to the council and took a seat on the end. Rye followed Wizard Thornberry's example, nodding to the wizards before he eased into his seat.

"Welcome, Sir Barley and Rye Fields," said the silver-haired wizard woman in sea-green robes who sat at the center of the council. On the high back of her chair, a brown owl blinked its orange eyes. As the woman spoke, the round walls echoed her soft voice, so it sounded as if she sat right in front of Rye instead of across the room. "Wizard Thornberry tells us you encountered a cursed ferryman and two enchanted villages on your journey through the Lost Forest. Will you please tell us all you can?"

SIX

The wizards asked many questions as Rye described the two villages and the ferryman. As they talked, Rye's fear of the wizards gradually faded. He wondered what amazing things these wizards could do, what mysteries they knew after a lifetime of searching the secrets of the Emerald Realms. He felt deeply honored to be speaking with them.

When Rye had finished, the silver-haired wizard woman said, "I believe all our suspicions have been confirmed."

"It certainly sounds like her work," another wizard agreed, this one all in black and who had a very intelligent-looking white pig sitting beside his chair.

"I have no other theories to put forth," said a third, tilting his head slightly to see past the bat dangling upside down from the brim of his hat.

The silver-haired wizard woman told Rye, "We believe the source of the problem is a certain troublesome fairy. She has a habit of disguising herself as an old beggar woman and asking anyone she meets for a favor. If someone is friendly to her, she grants them a gift or a wish. If someone is rude or unkind, she curses them. It sounds as if this fairy has visited these two villages and your ferryman, and that they have done something to offend her. In the case of the villages, they were probably helpful to her at first, which explains their magical tablecloths and sheep, but she often finds a way to be offended so that she can curse her victims in the end."

The wizard in black robes said, "We've appealed to the Fairy Court against her, but they have already banished her to Lost Forest. They believe she's no longer their responsibility."

"What can be done, then?" Rye asked.

The silver-haired wizard woman continued, "If you wish to help, you must go back to the villages and find out what they did to offend the fairy. Tell them they must make amends. She is bound by fairy law and can't harm them unless they owe her something. If you call her name, she will come. Then they can make their restitution, though you must warn them to be very, very careful not to offend her again."

A tall wizard in green, whose bushy hair reminded Rye of gray moss and whose collar had four finger-long yellow spider legs peeking out from under it, took a quill from the small table beside him. "I will write her name for you. We dare not speak it here. It is a dangerous thing to call on such a fairy. Do not say her name until the right time comes."

Rye was about to explain that he didn't know how to read, but when the wizard with the spider handed him the piece of paper with a single word written on it, he recognized all the letters and knew how they sounded. The name began with an "M" and an "e" like in "majesty," then "l" and "i" and "s" like in "illustrious" and then ended with "m" and "a" like majesty again. Melisma.

"I can read this!" Rye said, excited. He wondered what other words he could work out if he tried.

"Don't read it now," warned the wizard with the golden wings. She had a surprisingly sweet voice. "Do not say her name until you've spoken to the villagers, or to your ferryman, and they're ready to do whatever is necessary to remove the offense."

Rye asked, "How will they know what they need to do?"

The silver-haired wizard woman said, "When you know the true story, the solution will be clear."

EPISODE SIX: MELISMA

ONE

Barley waited impatiently while the wizards told Rye how to help the villagers and the ferryman they'd met in Lost Forest. As soon as the wizards seemed to be done, Barley jumped out of his chair. "Please, can you tell us what to do about the nix in our well?"

The wizards invited Barley to explain his trouble with the nix, so he gave them the whole story, acting it out as he spoke. He showed them how he'd slashed right through the nix with his sword, and told them that the nix hadn't cared one bit. Then he showed them how Rye had almost trapped the nix in the magically waterproofed boot. The wizards were very impressed by that. Even though it hadn't worked, they said it had been a very clever thing to do. Rye smiled, looking pleased with himself. Barley finished by acting out the tug-of-war between the nix and the rest of the village, which the villagers had lost.

The council's only advice was the same as Wizard Thornberry's. Dig a new well.

Barley sighed and sank back into his chair. He could have thought of that himself. They'd come all this way for nothing.

"Now that we've done our best to answer your questions, will you please tell us of your adventures last summer?" the wizard with the yellow spider asked.

Barley told the story, reluctantly at first, but then with growing enthusiasm when he saw how interested the wizards were in the magic sword, the witch, Lost Castle, the Dragon of the Deep, and Rye's friend, the selkie. The wizards especially wanted to know how Rye had tricked and banished the dragon from the Emerald Realms. Rye had to help out with that part of the story, since Barley hadn't seen it for himself.

As Rye finished the last details of his encounter with the dragon, the silver-haired wizard woman who seemed to be in charge of everything asked, "Rye Fields, have you ever thought of becoming a wizard?"

"I couldn't," Rye said, almost laughing. "I don't have any magic."

"Wizard magic isn't something you have," said a wizard in brown robes with a badger dozing at his feet. "It's something you learn."

"What you *do* have is the ability to see the opportunities before you and quickly choose the one that will lead where you desire," said a wizard who had her hand resting on the head of a gray wolf. "That's a most valuable skill for a wizard, and something far more difficult to teach than magic itself."

Barley stared at Rye. Rye didn't want to be a wizard, did he? Poke around in this old tower all his life, staring at books instead of riding around the countryside with his brother and having adventures as a pair of bold knights?

Rye looked down at the floor for a moment. "Thank you," he said, giving the council of wizards a regretful smile, "but no. I want to be a knight, like my brother."

Barley breathed a sigh of relief, then grinned at Rye.

The council seemed disappointed, but they nodded and smiled.

"If it is a knight you wish to be, we are sure you will be an excellent one," said the wizard with the badger.

The silver-haired wizard woman nodded her head. "Whatever you choose to do, you will do well."

TWO

All of the apprentice wizards, and many of the master wizards as well, came out to wish Barley and Rye a safe journey home. The cook loaded their saddlebags with hard biscuits and dried beef—glamoured to seem like sugared pastries, soft rolls, and a variety of juicy roasted meats. Briar came with her lion, Algernon, who purred when Barley rubbed his thick brown mane. Wizard Thornberry brought the flower Prince Aster had left behind.

Before Barley and Rye mounted their horses, Wizard Thornberry said, "I have something to give you."

"We really don't want the flower," Barley said. "I'm sure you can keep it."

Wizard Thornberry chuckled. "If you will remember, before Prince Aster ran off, I told him this flower *was* an ordinary flower. While that is true, I have since confirmed my suspicions that it no longer *is* an ordinary flower. The heartbroken tears of a young prince have powerful curse-breaking properties, and after being watered by them for a year and a day, the prince's zinnia is hardly ordinary."

"I thought you said the flower wasn't the Princess Zinnia," Barley said.

"The prince's zinnia. The zinnia belonging to the prince. This lovely blossom is a variety of flower called a zinnia, and it formerly belonged to a prince. Therefore I have decided to call it the prince's zinnia," Wizard Thornberry explained.

"Oh," Barley said.

"That *is* confusing," Rye said, with a sympathetic glance at Barley.

"At any rate, I was unable to tell the prince before he galloped off that his tears might not have been entirely wasted. As I suspected, the petals of this flower can protect against dark magic and break curses that have to do with matters of the heart. I will give one to each of you, and also another one that you should give to Prince Aster if you meet him again. If his true love is cursed, the petal should restore her."

"We shall gladly do this task," Barley said, doing his best to sound like a brave knight who had been charged with a dangerous quest, instead of just a boy who had been asked to give a flower petal to a prince.

"Wizard Thornberry?" Rye asked. "Do you think these petals would help the villages and the ferryman? Would you be willing to spare a few more?"

Wizard Thornberry smiled and shook his head. "I'm sorry, my boy, but these petals work only when true love is at stake. I doubt they would help your friends in Lost Forest." He plucked three petals from the flower, and Briar wrapped each one in its own small square of silk. Barley tucked two of them in the pouch at his belt, and Rye took the third for himself.

"I think now we owe you a debt," Rye said as he shook Wizard Thornberry's hand.

Wizard Thornberry said, "No, my boy. You owe us nothing. You have brought us much knowledge. The things you have told us will be studied for years to come. And Rye, if you should ever change your mind about becoming a wizard, we would be delighted to have you. Any one of us would be honored to take you as an apprentice."

"Thank you," Rye said. He glanced at Barley, then up at the tower of Wizard's Keep. Barley wasn't sure, but he thought maybe Rye was thinking he might like to be a wizard, and that he might want to stay at Wizard's Keep and never leave again.

Worried, Barley held his breath until Rye said, "Goodbye, Wizard Thornberry. Thank you for everything."

"Yes, thank you!" Barley agreed, very happy that Rye would be coming home with him after all.

THREE

Barley and Rye found the fisherman and his son waiting for them in their boat at the docks in Frogsfoot. The fisherman and his son hadn't seen Prince Aster, who must have hired someone else to take him across.

Late that afternoon, after sailing to the far side of the lake, Barley and Rye asked the people of Frogshead if they had seen the prince. No one had. It wasn't too surprising, as the prince had sailed from Frogsfoot at dusk and would have arrived at Frogshead in the middle of the night. Barley and Rye could only hope that he'd gone home the same way they'd come, and that they might catch up to him on their way.

The weather was fine, so Barley and Rye set out along the lakeshore and camped that night where the path to Appledale led into the Lost Forest. As they rode along the path the next day, they searched for signs of Prince Aster. Now and then, they would see a hoofprint in the dirt that showed them someone had come that way recently, but they couldn't be sure it was the prince.

After three days' journey, they reached the village of Appledale. When Rye told the shepherd girls he had learned how to break the curse on their apple tree, the girls ran to tell all of their friends and neighbors. The whole village gathered around the leafless tree at the center of the valley and waited to hear what Rye had to say.

"The wizards told us there is a fairy in Lost Forest who disguises herself as an old beggar woman and deals out blessings and curses," Rye said. "They think she is the one who has given you sheep that make gold and also cursed your apple tree. Did you see anyone like that? Can you tell me the story?"

The villagers shook their heads, confused, but the shepherd girls' faces turned pink and they gave each other uncomfortable glances.

"Do you know something?" Rye asked the shepherd girls.

"There may have been an old beggar woman," the black-haired shepherdess said.

"She might have come to us one morning as we were tending the sheep," said the brown-haired one. "Last fall, maybe." She nervously twisted one of the many gold rings around her finger.

"I knew there was something off about her!" said the red-haired shepherdess. "She told us she was hungry and wanted one of our sweet apples. So we went and picked her one, and gave it to her. She said that since we'd been so kind to her, we could have one wish in return. None of us believed her. We thought she was a batty old hag. We wanted to humor her, though, and since we'd always been so poor, we wished for some gold."

The black-haired shepherdess said, "And then the old beggar woman said we could have all the gold we wanted. We could get it from the sheep."

"You can imagine how we were trying not to laugh," the brown-haired shepherdess said. "But then she showed us how to do it. We were so excited, making piles and piles of gold, that we didn't notice when the old woman went away."

"We haven't seen her since," the red-haired shepherdess said.

"Did you ever thank her?" Rye asked.

The three shepherd girls shook their heads and looked down at their golden shoes.

FOUR

After the story was told, even Barley knew what the shepherd girls needed to do to break the curse on their apple tree. They had to thank the old beggar woman, who had obviously been the fairy in disguise. The villagers talked it over and decided it wasn't enough simply to say thank you. They wanted to give the fairy a gift. They worked all that day and through the night, beating and shaping gold into a beautiful crown decorated with golden apple blossoms. When the crown was finished, the whole village stood around the tree. The shepherd girls told Rye they were ready for him to call the fairy.

Rye studied the paper the wizards had given him, then said a word Barley had never heard before.

Everyone held their breath and waited.

Nothing happened.

Rye tried saying the word again, but still the fairy didn't come.

"Maybe I'm not saying it right," Rye said. He picked up a stick and began to scratch in the dirt under the tree. The villagers gathered around to watch him. "Oh," he said.

"Maybe it's not like 'a' in 'majesty,' but like 'a' in 'far.' Melisma."

The air hummed with a faint sound, like the chimes Barley had heard ringing the hours in King's Town. Wind stirred the grass, then grew stronger until the branches of the bare apple tree swayed and creaked against each other. The chimes swelled so loud, Barley wanted to cover his ears. A bright light appeared high overhead as if a star had woken in the daytime. It drifted down like a snowflake until it hovered a few feet in front of Rye, who shaded his eyes against the glare while the wind whipped his traveling cloak. With a final clang of bells, the light burst and became a graceful girl with black hair and lovely acorn-brown skin. A silvery-blue gown draped down to her ankles, and her thin, glassy wings swirled with rainbows. Barley thought she was the most beautiful creature he had ever seen until he looked into her ice-green eyes and saw no kindness there. His heart chilled, and he was afraid.

The wind died to a whisper. The fairy said, "Yes?" as if she'd been standing there the whole time and Rye had only spoken her name to get her attention.

Rye seemed to have forgotten how to speak. He gestured toward the three shepherd girls, who cowered together in front of the crowd of cringing villagers.

The black-haired shepherd girl gripped the golden crown in her shaking hands. "W-we only wanted to thank you," she stammered.

"For the gold," said the brown-haired one.

"We've made you a gift." The red-haired shepherd girl gave the black-haired one a shove toward the fairy.

The fairy smiled and took the crown from the terrified shepherd girl. She turned it over in her hands as if admiring the delicate golden blossoms. Then she placed the crown on her head. "You're welcome," the fairy said. She passed her gaze over the crowd of villagers, then turned her attention on Rye. Her jaw tightened, and her eyes flashed a fierce warning. Even standing next to Rye, Barley could feel the force of her anger. He felt a quick urge to draw his sword and protect his brother. Rye took a step back, watching the fairy as if waiting to see what she would do next.

With a sudden movement that made the villagers gasp in fear, the fairy pointed at the bare apple tree. Green leaves and white blossoms surged along the branches. Dead winter became a living springtime in a single instant.

"Thank you," Rye said.

The fairy made a displeased grunt in her throat, then vanished in a bright flash of light.

FIVE

With the fairy gone, all the villagers breathed a sigh of relief. They turned and gazed up with smiles of wonder at their blossoming tree. Someone laughed, a few of them clapped, and several joined hands in a circle and danced in a wide ring with the tree at the center.

Barley wasn't smiling. "I don't like that fairy," he said to Rye. "Maybe we shouldn't call her again."

"I don't like her either," Rye said. "But I promised I'd help the other village, and the ferryman too."

Sobbing with joy, the black-haired shepherdess threw her arms around Rye. "Thank you so much!" she said, squeezing him tight. "Our tree is blooming again!"

"You're welcome," Rye said. He patted her on the shoulder, giving Barley a startled, silent plea for help.

"We have a gift for you too," the brown-haired shepherdess said, and pressed a kiss on Rye's cheek. His face turned pink.

"We want to give you one of our sheep." The red-haired shepherdess handed Rye a golden rope that was tied around the neck of a woolly white sheep.

"Oh, no, we couldn't take one of your sheep," Rye said, clearly flustered. He tried to give the rope back.

"Please," the black-haired shepherd girl said, finally letting go of Rye. "It's the least we can do."

"We'll take it," Barley said. "And thank you!"

Six

Barley tied the sheep's golden rope to his horse's saddle, and they rode away through the forest. The golden bell around the sheep's neck made a cheerful tinkling sound as they went.

"This solves all sorts of problems," Barley said, happy and excited. "I'll have enough gold to finish the castle and pay the taxes, and we can even get you a nice sword of your own, Rye!"

Rye stayed silent, thinking his own thoughts.

After they made camp that night, Barley opened the last saddlebag the cook at Wizard's Keep had packed for them. He was surprised to find it mostly empty, as he hadn't opened it since they'd left the keep. At the bottom, something hissed up at him and spurted a thin yellow flame. A scarlet head shot toward him, snapping its teeth. Barley yelped and jumped back.

Rye dropped the sticks he'd been collecting and came running. "What happened?" he asked.

"Dragon!" Barley pointed. "One of those pygmy dragons from Wizard's Keep. It stowed away in my saddlebag. And look! It's eaten our food!" Barley had seen the cook pack that bag to the top, but now only a few pastries, squished and with a bite or two taken out of them, stuck to the inside of the bag.

"Shoo!" Rye said to the dragon. "Get out of there!"

The dragon grabbed a pastry in its mouth, then shot out of the bag and flapped its way into a nearby tree. Barley picked up the bag, shook his head sadly, then pulled out three squashed and dragon-nibbled pastries. He gave one to Rye, kept one for himself, and broke the third in half for them to share.

"We'll get a good meal tomorrow," Rye said when they'd licked every last crumb off their fingers. "The table-cloths, remember?"

Barley sighed. That didn't help with the fact that he was hungry now.

As Rye worked on starting the fire, Barley thought he heard something moving in the forest, far off at first, but coming closer. Leaves rustled and twigs snapped like they were giving way for a herd of large, clumsy animals that was passing through. The sound came so close that Rye stood up from tending the fire and peered into the forest to see what it might be.

A dense patch of bushes hid whatever was making the noise. The horses snorted nervously, stamped their feet, and pulled on the ropes that tethered them to a tree. The sheep jerked against its rope and dug into the ground with its hooves. Seeing the animals' eyes stretched wide and white-rimmed made Barley's heart pound. He drew his sword as he and Rye backed away from the bushes.

A huge head burst into the clearing, sickly yellow, with eye stalks like a slug, and a gaping, sticky, toothless mouth. It reared up and roared with a voice like a crowd of men and beasts all howling at once. Forever after, whenever Barley was at a noisy fair or in a clamoring city market, the sound would take him back to this awful moment.

The horses screamed as the monster charged forward into the clearing. It had a long body made of segments, each one like a different animal. Black hide with horse's hooves, gray hair with wolf paws, duck feathers with webbed feet, fish scales with spiny fins, snakeskin with no legs at all, but most horrible were the parts in human clothing with human arms or legs. The part closest to the monster's head wore a red jacket with gold buttons and black trim. Prince Aster's jacket.

"Rye, look!" Barley wailed. "It got Prince Aster!"

The parataxis had found them.

EPISODE SEVEN: THE PARATAXIS

ONE

"Cut the horses loose!" Rye shouted as the parataxis surged into the clearing.

Barley ran and slashed the ropes with his sword. The horses tore themselves free. Barley darted behind the tree as the parataxis rushed by. It chased after the horses that galloped, screaming in fright, off into the woods. Barley chopped through the sheep's golden rope where it was tied to the tree. With the rope no longer holding it, the sheep stumbled forward and fell to the ground. Before the sheep could stand up, the parataxis doubled back, coiling its long body with its stomping, crawling, waving feet. A giant yellow bird claw on a black-feathered section grabbed the sheep and held it pinned to the ground. The parataxis's mouth opened wide, stretching strands of yellow goo between its jaws.

"No!" Barley shouted and charged at the parataxis, swinging his sword. He slashed at the parataxis's body, but it coiled away out of his reach, dragging the sheep with it. The parataxis's head shot toward the frantically bleating sheep, and the open mouth slurped it in. With one last gulp, the parataxis sucked down the end of the golden rope and turned to face Barley.

Something grabbed Barley's ankle. He stumbled and looked down. A human arm wearing a sleeve of tattered brown leather had reached out from the side of the parataxis and clutched his boot. Barley tried to slash the arm with his sword, but a sharp hoof kicked him in the back, knocking him to the ground. Rye shouted, but Barley couldn't see him. The coils of the parataxis curled in on Barley, flapping, beating, clawing, and kicking. Barley's sword was wrenched from his hand. Fingers, sharp claws, and even a slimy foot like a giant frog's held him down as the parataxis's sluglike head rose over him. Eyes black and empty as a starless night stared at Barley with bottomless hunger.

Instead of opening its mouth to swallow Barley, the head shook itself. Eye stalks contracted, drawing the black eye-globes down into the parataxis's head. Its jowls wriggled, and the mouth opened and closed like a gasping fish. Barley felt the grip on his ankle weaken. He jerked one arm out from under a bear's paw and tore the frog's foot off his neck. Two human hands grabbed his other arm and dragged him free of the parataxis's coils. Barley stumbled to his feet as Rye pulled him out of the parataxis's reach. His body ached from bruises and smarted from scratches. He looked for some direction they could run, but the monster had wound itself around the clearing, surrounding them.

The two brothers stood together, gasping, as a shiver ran along the parataxis's whole length. The parataxis laid its head down, and the mouth let out a groan. With a slimy *slop*, a woolly white segment slid out of the base of the neck. Barley's stomach lurched and the pastry he'd eaten only a few minutes before rose up in his throat.

Now Prince Aster's jacket had a section of woolly sheep body coming out the top. Two wobbly sheep legs pawed at the ground, trying to stand up. A loop of gold rope with a golden bell hung around the sheep wool at the base of the parataxis's neck.

"Get your sword," Rye said. He dashed toward the monster's head.

"Rye! What are you doing?" Barley shouted.

"Sword!" Rye said. He jumped on the sheep section's back and held tight to the rope. The parataxis's eyestalks stretched and whipped around frantically as if trying to see what had grabbed on to it.

Barley snatched his sword from under a drooping hairy pig belly. Lizard claws raked at him, but he pulled free. Up at the front, the parataxis shook and flailed, trying to throw Rye off.

"Ring tickle rit rickle!" Rye shouted. He hooked one elbow through the rope, and with his other hand, he rubbed the sheep's wool. A shower of gold coins flew everywhere as the parataxis swung its neck, trying to shake Rye off. All along the parataxis, human hands grabbed for the coins and stuffed them into their pockets, but other segments coiled toward Rye, trying to reach him with claws, paws, and talons. Trying to fight his way through to help his brother,

Barley rushed in and plunged his sword deep into a scaly fish segment. His sword trailed yellow slime as he drew it out. Barley turned and chopped down hard on the back of a slippery frog part. The blade cut deep, and the parataxis's body curled away, oozing yellow.

The claws of a bat's wing grabbed Barley's sword arm. Barley tore the claws off with his free hand, only to be knocked off his feet as another part of the parataxis slammed into his legs. Barley tried to get up, but hairy black paws on his arms pinned him facedown. Scaly claws grasped his legs, and insect hooks latched onto his boots.

"Barley!" He heard Rye call his name. Barley turned his head to see the parataxis make a tremendous lurch, snapping its neck like a whip. Rye lost hold of the rope and flew into the air. The heavy thud when Rye hit the ground struck Barley like a blow.

"Rye!" Barley shouted. "Get up! Run!"

Rye didn't move. The front end of the parataxis crawled toward him on sheep legs, Prince Aster's human hands, fish fins, and the limbs of every other poor creature the parataxis had swallowed.

"Rye!" Barley shouted again, fighting to free himself so he could do something to keep the parataxis from swallowing Rye. The parataxis held him fast.

Rye sat up, but he didn't get to his feet. He looked at Barley and said, terrified but determined, "While it's growing, cut off its head."

"Run!" Barley pleaded.

Rye never looked away from Barley, never saw the parataxis raise the first four sections of its horrible long body, never saw it lift its open mouth high above his head, never saw it come down.

"No!" Barley screamed.

Two

Barley wrenched himself out of the parataxis's weakened grip. He stood up, sobbing. Gripping his sword, he ran alongside the trembling patchwork body. Like it had when it swallowed the sheep, the parataxis pulled its eyestalks in and worked its sticky mouth. Something was different, though. The monster gagged, writhed, and threw its head onto the ground, moaning with a hundred voices of animal pain. Barley refused to feel sorry for it. The parataxis had eaten his brother.

Barley raised his sword and charged the last few strides with a roar. Rye would never be a part of this awful beast. Barley would not let that happen. He swung his sword down on the monster's slimy yellow neck. The blade sliced clean through, and the head rolled to the side, mouth to the ground, eyestalks popping out limp and dead.

Barley dropped his sword and fell to his hands and knees. The long, wriggling body of the parataxis convulsed, headless, all around him. Barley closed his eyes and wept. Tears for the way Rye had let the parataxis swallow him to give Barley a chance to slay it. Tears for the sword Barley had meant to get for Rye, but now never would. Tears for all the adventures they'd never have together. Tears for having to go home alone and tell Mother and Father what had happened.

Something warm and woolly nudged him, and a bell tinkled near his ear. Barley wrapped his arms around the sheep's neck and cried into its wool. "I'm so sorry you got eaten!" he sobbed.

"Sir Barley?" Prince Aster's voice made Barley look up. The clearing was full of animals, shaking themselves and standing. A woman screamed at finding herself sitting next to a big black bear. The bear lumbered off quickly into the forest as if he were just as frightened of her. Birds flapped into the sky, snakes crawled into the underbrush, deer pranced off through the trees, wolves, pigs, sheep, goats, and horses trotted away. About a dozen confused, curious people, along with Prince's Aster's big black warhorse, gathered around Barley and Prince Aster. Barley recognized the brown leather coat of the arm that had grabbed him, now worn by a man with a short gray beard and a kind face. These were all the people the parataxis had eaten! They'd been freed, along with Prince Aster and all the animals.

But what about Rye?

"What happened?" asked the woman who had been next to the bear.

"Where are we?" asked the old man in the leather jacket.

"And why are my pockets full of gold?" asked a young minstrel with a lute strapped to his back. He pulled his hand out of his vest pocket and showed everyone a gold coin.

"There's more gold on the ground!" said a little girl.

A faint sound came from the severed head of the parataxis, like someone shouting with their face in a bucket of tar. Barley turned to see the side bulging. Something was trying to push its way out.

"It's still alive!" someone shrieked.

The sound came again, a muffled, "Help!"

"Rye!" Barley jumped up. He shoved on the massive severed head, trying to roll it so the mouth wasn't pinned shut beneath it. The prince ran to help him, and soon everyone was pushing, pulling, and tugging until the head rolled onto its side. A hand covered in yellow slime reached out of the sagging mouth. Barley grabbed it and pulled a shaking, sputtering Rye out onto the ground. As soon as Rye climbed free and stood up, Barley tackled him with a hug.

"You're alive!" Barley said, squeezing his brother hard. He'd noticed before that Rye had grown taller than him over the winter, but he hadn't realized how much taller until that moment. Rye's shoulder was almost higher than Barley's nose.

"Somehow." Rye sounded like he hadn't expected to be alive either.

"Don't leave me like that!" Barley said, sobbing again. "Not ever. You can't leave me. I can't do this without you. Promise you won't!"

THREE

Rye didn't say anything, but held his brother tight until Barley calmed down. Rye couldn't make such a promise, and he knew it. Even if he wasn't planning on going away to become a knight, other things could happen. He couldn't promise Barley that they'd always be together.

Barley let out one last ragged sigh, and they both let go.

"You're covered with slime!" Barley said, indignant, as if Rye had gotten slime on Barley's jacket on purpose.

"You are too." Rye gave him a friendly shove, putting his sticky hand on a clean patch on Barley's shoulder.

Barley laughed, his blue eyes extra bright with tears.

"How did you slay the parataxis?" Prince Aster asked. "I fought it with all my strength, but it overwhelmed and consumed me."

Barley rubbed his face on a clean part of his sleeve, then said, "Rye let it eat him. It had grabbed me, but then after it swallowed Rye, while it was busy trying to make a new piece of itself, I got away from it and cut off its head."

"I noticed that when it ate the sheep it stopped fighting," Rye said, raking at the goo in his hair. "Not for long, but long enough." Every breath of fresh air surprised him. Moments ago, he'd been suffocating, crushed as if inside a giant grinding fist that wanted to mash him to a pulp. He didn't know what had kept his bones from snapping to splinters.

"That was very brave, Rye," Prince Aster said. "You and your brother have saved my life and the lives of all of these people. If you wish to be a knight, come to my father's court. Even if he doesn't grant you knighthood on the spot, I will see that you are made squire to one of the best knights in the land. Then, when you are of age, a Knight of the Land Far Away you shall be."

"Good for you, Rye!" Barley said. "You've done your brave deed." Then he gasped as if he'd just remembered something very important. "Oh! Prince Aster! I have something for you!"

While Barley told Prince Aster what Wizard Thornberry had said about the flower petals, Rye took out his own petal. When he unfolded the square of cloth, there was no petal. Only a little bit of white ash.

"Look, Barley." Rye showed his brother the empty cloth. "I think the petal helped keep me safe. It's gone now. But how did it work? Wizard Thornberry said the petals would only break a curse if it had to do with true love."

"You must be in love with one of those shepherd girls from Appledale," Barley teased. "Which one is it? The one who kissed you?" Barley giggled and darted away as Rye tried to smack him.

Prince Aster unfolded his cloth. A bright orange petal

lay in its folds. "It may have been for my sake that your petal freed us all from the parataxis, Rye," Prince Aster said, his voice catching with emotion. "And I shall use this petal to free my true love from whatever dark enchantment binds her."

"I wonder what I'll use mine for," Barley said. He unfolded his cloth enough to see his own petal still safe inside, then wrapped it up carefully and put it away.

Four

The next day, Barley, Rye, and all the people they'd freed from the parataxis reached the village of Crystal Springs. They had no supplies and had traveled on foot, except for the little girl who rode on Prince Aster's horse while he walked alongside, and so everyone was very hungry and tired when they arrived.

The villagers were overjoyed to hear that the parataxis had been slain and that the wizards had told Rye how to restore the water in their spring. To celebrate, they brought their tables outside, shook their tablecloths, and shared a meal with their guests. As they ate together, Rye told them what had happened at Appledale. Then he asked the villagers if any of them had seen an old beggar woman who might have been the fairy in disguise.

"Yes, we saw her," said a little boy, the one who had been in the hut where Barley, Rye, and Prince Aster had stopped the first time they came to the village. "My sister and my grandmother and I met her when we were gathering sticks in the forest."

"She said she was thirsty and wanted a drink of water," the boy's sister said.

"I sent the children to run and fetch a cup from the house, fill it at the spring, and bring it to her," the grandmother said. "After she drank the water, she asked if she could do anything to return our kindness."

"My brother asked if she had any food," the sister said. "It was a silly thing to ask. It was obvious the old woman didn't have anything."

"We were hungry," the brother said, defending himself. "I told her the whole village was hungry."

The grandmother said, "She said the strangest thing then. She told us that all we had to do was shake our tablecloths three times before we laid them on our tables, and we would have all the food we wanted. I didn't believe her."

"I didn't either," the little girl said.

"I did!" the boy said. "I ran back to the house, got the tablecloth, shook it three times and laid it on the table, and there was a feast!"

"I went chasing after him," the sister said. "By the time I got there, he was stuffing his face. The whole village came crowding around our hut, wondering where we had gotten the food. I told them to try their own tablecloths, and soon everyone was feasting and celebrating our good luck."

"That's what they were doing when I found them," the grandmother said. "We were all so happy, eating away, that we forgot the old beggar woman. That was, until the rich food made us thirsty. I sent my granddaughter to the spring with a pitcher, but she came back with the pitcher empty. Our spring had dried up."

"We knew it had something to do with her," the girl said. "But she was gone. We never saw her again."

"Yes," the grandmother said. "If all we have to do is thank her, we'll be more than glad to do it."

FIVE

The villagers of Crystal Springs decided to do more than thank the fairy. They prepared a special feast in her honor. All that day, they worked to build a bower and hang it with garlands of spring wildflowers. Underneath the bower, they placed a chair for the fairy and lined up the tables in front of it. Everyone dressed in their very finest, and Rye worked hard to brush the last of the dried parataxis slime from his hair and clothes. At last, around sundown, when everything was ready, the villagers told Rye to call the fairy.

"Maybe I should call her this time," Barley said.

"Why?" Rye asked.

"I don't know. She seemed awfully mad at you last time. Maybe if someone else calls her this time, she won't be so mad at you."

"Barley, I don't want you in trouble with that fairy," Rye said.

"I'm not scared!" Barley said. "Let me call her."

Rye nodded. "Go ahead, then."

Barley opened his mouth, then closed it and frowned. "What was her name?"

Rye sighed. "Melisma."

With a crash of bells and a furious wind that sent the villagers scrambling to catch flying flower garlands and hold the bower in place, a brilliant light descended out of the evening sky. The light burst into a million sparks of white and the fairy stood there on the grass. Her pale green eyes flashed cold, and a thin, dangerous smile played on her lips.

"Yes?" she asked.

While the villagers hurried to put everything back in order after the sudden windstorm, the old grandmother came forward. "We would like to apologize most humbly for not thanking you sooner. You have bestowed great bounty on our village, and to show our gratitude, we have prepared a feast in your honor. Will you please join us?"

The fairy's smile grew wider, but no less dangerous. "I accept."

SIX

The outdoor feast reminded Rye of the night last summer when everyone in Humble Village gathered to celebrate the Lord of Lost Castle's defeat. The food was delicious, the villagers were friendly and welcoming, and the minstrel who had been rescued from the parataxis wasn't half bad either. The minstrel sang a tragic ballad about a lonely princess trapped in a castle on top of a glass mountain, which made Prince Aster cry, and then a funny song about a battle of wits between a pixie and a cat, which made everyone laugh. Rye would have enjoyed it if the fairy hadn't kept turning her icy-green eyes to glare in his direction. He dreaded having to summon her one last time to help the ferryman, but he told himself that once that was over, he would be done with her forever. He just had to be careful, that's all. She couldn't hurt him unless he offended her. That's what the wizards had said.

After everyone had eaten so much that they were tired of eating, the fairy stood up from her place of honor at the table. She walked lightly over the grass, wings gleaming in the moonlight, until she came to stand by the dry basin of the spring. The villagers and their guests followed at a careful distance. The fairy bent over the basin and touched the dry rocks with her delicate fingers. Shimmering darkness rose up, as if clear night sky filled the basin. A fresh stream of sweet smelling water burbled over the stones and trickled down the grassy channel toward the distant river.

The villagers cheered, clapped, and called out their thanks to the fairy. A merry tune sang out from the minstrel's lute, and everyone began to dance, except for Rye and Melisma. She turned to face him, her face mocking and haughty, eyebrows up, mouth down, as if to say, *Was that what you wanted, you little fool?*

"Thank you," Rye said with a nod.

Melisma narrowed her eyes and vanished with a dull clink.

EPISODE EIGHT: THE LOST FOREST INN

ONE

The next day, before Barley and Rye set out on their journey home, the grateful villagers of Crystal Springs presented them with one of their magic tablecloths. Rye didn't think it was right to take such a valuable gift when all they'd done was give them a little advice, but Barley couldn't have been more pleased.

"Now we'll have all the food and all the money we could possibly want," Barley said as they walked through the forest toward the river. "We'll never have any problems again! I'm sure no one back home will mind that we didn't figure out how to get the nix out of the well. At least, not once we show them what this sheep and this tablecloth can do. No one will need to farm anymore, and we could hire the workmen to dig *ten* more wells, anywhere in the village that we want. My castle should have a nice well of its own, don't you think?"

Prince Aster, who rode slowly beside them, nodded. "It is a wise thing to have a well within your own castle walls. If you should be under siege, you will never want for water."

"We won't want for food, either, and with gold from the sheep, we can probably pay the soldiers who are surrounding us to go away and leave us alone."

"I wonder if that would make a good ballad," the minstrel said. "The Siege of Humble Castle." He had come along with Barley, Rye, and Prince Aster because he wanted to learn the details of their adventures so he could make them into songs. The other people who had been freed from the parataxis had either stayed in Crystal Springs or set off for their homes in other directions. After humming a few experimental notes to himself, the minstrel strummed on his lute and sang, *"Sir Barley was a brave, true knight, and a brave, true knight was he. He had a woolly, woolly sheep that shed gold coins for free . . ."*

Rye felt glad too, in a way, because with the magic sheep and the magic tablecloth, Barley wouldn't have any trouble taking care of Humble Village on his own. There would be no need for Rye to stay and help him. In fact, Rye thought he might not stop in Humble Village at all, but instead go on with Prince Aster to King's Town to see if King Hugric would make him a knight.

But first, Rye had promised to help the ferryman, and that meant calling Melisma one last time.

TWO

When they reached the White River, the ferryman came out of his hut and used his pole to push his ferry to the shore. "What news, friends?" he asked in his sad, faded voice. "Did you discover some way to free me from this unending task?"

"The wizards said there is a fairy in Lost Forest who disguises herself as an old beggar woman," Rye said. "She asks those she meets to help her, and if they refuse or offend her in any way, she curses them. Do you remember seeing anyone like that?"

The ferryman shook his head. "I don't remember ever taking an old beggar woman across the river."

Rye said, "This would have been before you had to take people across. She may have been the one who cursed you to have to do this."

The ferryman sighed and leaned on his pole. "It has been so long. I can't recall what happened before."

"What a sad song that would be!" the minstrel said. He plucked slowly on his lute. *The ferryman of the White River had a beard as white as the foam . . .*

"Please, not now," Prince Aster said.

"Sorry." The minstrel hung his lute back on his shoulder with a twang.

"The wizards said not to call the fairy unless we knew what to do to remove the offense," Rye said. "Can you remember anything? Please try."

"I will take you across while I'm thinking," the ferryman said.

The ferryman took Prince Aster and his horse first, and then Barley, Rye, and the minstrel. When they had all reached the other side of the river, the ferryman still hadn't been able to remember if he'd seen the old beggar woman.

"She might have cursed him to forget," Barley said.

Rye had been thinking the same thing. "We'll have to call her and ask her."

"Do you want me to?" Barley asked.

Rye shook his head. "I'm the one who promised to help. I'll call her. Everyone stand back, and don't say or do anything that might offend the fairy."

Barley motioned for Rye to step away from everyone else. When they'd gone a few paces into the trees, Barley said, keeping his voice down so the others wouldn't hear, "Rye, are you sure you want to call the fairy? We don't even know what the ferryman needs to do to remove his curse. And besides, you already saved Prince Aster from the parataxis. The king's going to knight you. I'm sure of it. You don't have to keep helping everyone we meet."

"I can't believe you said that," Rye said. "What kind of a knight would I be if I only helped people when I thought it would help me?" It was true that when Rye had first offered to help the ferryman, he'd been hoping it would give him a brave deed to do, but now, even though he'd already done his brave deed, he had his word to keep.

"I'm sorry." Barley glanced back at the ferryman, then stared up anxiously into Rye's face. "It's only that I'm . . . worried."

"Me too." Rye put his hand on Barley's shoulder and led him back to the river.

Rye stood by the ferryman as Barley, Prince Aster, and the minstrel watched from several paces away. Prince Aster gave Rye a solemn, encouraging nod. The minstrel had an eager grin on his face. Rye could imagine him happily working out the lines for a song about how Rye Fields was cursed by an angry fairy.

Rye took a deep breath and then asked as humbly as he could, "Melisma?"

A crashing clang like lightning striking a bell tower blasted through the woods, and a burst of wind blew the minstrel's hat right off his head and set the ferryman's platform rocking. Blinding light flashed and the fairy appeared, hands on her hips, glaring at Rye.

"Yes?" she demanded with a voice as terrible as a dragon's roar.

When the echoes of her voice had died down, Rye swallowed hard. He tried not to let his voice crack as he said, "I beg your pardon for calling you again, but if this poor ferryman has offended you in any way, he'd like to apologize and make amends. The trouble is, he can't remember anything that happened before he was cursed. Will you help him, please?"

"Ah, so you *can* say something other than, 'Thank you.'" The fairy twined her fingers and made a mock curtsy.

Rye thought it best to keep his mouth shut.

"I had nothing to do with this curse." The fairy sneered. "This is an old, old curse. Far older than he is." She pointed to the ferryman. "My magic can't touch it, but since I'm in a very generous mood today, very generous, I'll tell you how to break it."

"I would be most grateful." The ferryman bowed low.

"The curse isn't on you," the fairy said. "It's on that pole. If you give it to someone else and they willingly take it, they'll have to ferry people across the river, and you'll be free."

The ferryman's tired old eyes lit up. "Yes, so it is! I remember now. I took the pole from the last ferryman. Yes, I did. I think . . . I think I was a king once. A long, long time ago."

"Thank you for telling him," Rye said. "Is there anything I can do to repay you?"

"Never. Call. Me. Again." With each word, the fairy stepped closer to Rye until her pretty little pointed nose was an inch from his face. A sweet scent of dewy honeysuckle nearly choked him. Her furious pale-green eyes flashed, and then she vanished with a sound like a dropped cauldron cracking on solid stone.

She didn't even need to ask. Rye never, ever wanted to see her again.

THREE

The travelers left the ferryman waiting for someone who would take his pole. That night as they made camp along the river, Barley thought Rye looked very pleased with himself when they overheard Prince Aster warning the minstrel about the talking squirrels that liked to steal feathered hats.

In the morning, they followed the river until it joined with the road, then followed the road to the Lost Forest Inn. The inn was a happy sight for Barley because it meant this adventure was nearly over. Soon he'd be home, and he could show his whole village the magical tablecloth and the sheep that made gold.

That night at the inn, guests packed the big room on the ground floor. Dwarves clambered over a giant's leg to join their group in the corner. On top of one table, dozens of tiny tables had been set up for a crowd of pixies who seemed to be celebrating a wedding.

"Look, Rye, pixies *are* real." Barley nudged Rye and pointed to the table. "But they're way too small to steal my shoes," he added, remembering last summer when Rye had hidden Barley's shoes and blamed it on the pixies.

"A lot of them working together could have done it," Rye said, watching the butterfly-winged bride and her dragonfly-winged groom smile at each other as they took their vows in front of a solemn moth-winged old pixie woman.

"It was you," Barley said flatly.

Rye gave him a teasing grin, as if to say, *Maybe, but let's see you prove it.*

Prince Aster adjusted his hat and gave Rye a very sharp look, but didn't say anything.

The minstrel took a spot at the corner of the hearth, right underneath the sack that hung from a spike in the wall, and started in on one of his new songs. Barley asked the toad and the swan if he, Rye, and Prince Aster, along with their sheep, could join their table.

"Of course," the toad said.

"Where's your friend the raven?" Barley asked as they sat down and the sheep settled by Barley's chair.

The swan said, "Her seven years' curse is almost up, so she's gone to see if her true love remembers her. If he has, she'll be freed. If not, she'll be a raven forever."

"How awful!" Barley said. "I hope he remembers."

"At least her curse has a possible end to it," the swan said. "Mine's permanent."

"How did your curse come about?" Prince Aster asked.

"I was throwing rocks at some swans. How was I to know it was the Swan King and his court? They cursed me to become a swan myself . . . for all eternity."

"Just for throwing rocks?" Barley asked. "That doesn't seem fair. Here, I wonder if this will help."

Barley took out his small square of silk and unfolded it. The orange flower petal lay in the middle.

"What is it?" the swan asked.

"A petal of the prince's zinnia," Barley said.

"A petal of the Princess Zinnia?" Prince Aster jumped up, furious. He slapped the tabletop. "The wizard said the flower was *not* my Princess Zinnia! Was he lying to me?"

"No, no!" Barley held his hands up. "The *prince's* zinnia! The zinnia that belonged to you, the prince. *Your* zinnia, not the Princess Zinnia."

"Oh." Prince Aster sank down in his chair. "Oh, I see."

Barley said to the swan, "This petal can break curses that have to do with true love. Try touching it."

The swan put a wingtip on the petal, but nothing happened. "I don't think my curse is the right kind to be broken by this charm," the swan said.

"How about you?" Barley asked the toad. "Are you in love with anyone?"

"Sadly, no." The toad picked up the petal in his front toes, then set it back down.

"Excuse me!" Willem came toward the table, waving his goose wing. "Excuse me, hello! Good to see you again, but I'm going to have to ask you to put that sheep in the stables. Unless it's a talking sheep, of course."

Barley shook his head and put his arms protectively around the sheep's neck.

Willem smiled, but firmly put one hand and one wing on his hips. "No livestock in the public room, terribly sorry. I hope it's not too much trouble."

"It doesn't talk, but it is magic," Barley said. "See? *Ring tickle rit rickle!"*

"Wait, Barley," Rye said.

Eager to show Willem what his magic sheep could do, Barley didn't wait. He raked his fingers through the sheep's wool, and a shower of coins tinkled down onto the wooden floor.

Everyone in the room fell silent, every pair of eyes on the pile of gold.

"There's plenty," Barley said. "Help yourselves."

All over the room, people jumped up, crowding toward Barley and his sheep. Barley grabbed the sheep around the middle and held it protectively in his lap as the crowd snatched at the coins.

"Here! Here! What's going on?" the innkeeper shouted from across the room.

"That boy's giving away gold coins!" someone responded.

"Settle down, everyone! Easy there!" the innkeeper called out. "One at a time! We don't want any trouble, now do we?"

Rye and Willem tried their best to keep the crowd from squashing Barley.

"Let's not be greedy now," Prince Aster said. "Perhaps one coin apiece?"

A couple of dwarves began to scuffle over the last few coins in the pile.

"That's enough! Everyone go sit down!" the innkeeper said. He glared at the two dwarves still squabbling. "You two, back off, or you're going in the sack!"

The dwarves immediately calmed down and backed away from each other, bowing to the innkeeper and apologizing.

"The sack?" Barley asked.

Willem pointed his wing at the sack hanging by the fireplace. "It's my father's magic sack. Anyone he tells to get in it pops inside and has to stay until he tells them they can come out. That's how he can have all sorts of customers in this place and still have so little trouble. If there's any fighting . . . POP! Into the sack!"

"Wow!" Barley said. "Can I borrow that sack? I could tell the nix to get inside it, and . . ."

"No, you can't," Willem said.

"Not even for a couple of days?"

"Don't even think about it," Willem said. "But you're right. It would be best to keep the sheep with you." Willem glanced over his shoulder at a shadowy corner of the inn where a few dim figures hunched around a table. Barley couldn't make out their faces, but he did catch the gleam of a single gold coin in the fingers of one of the men. "I don't like the look of that crew over there, but it's our policy to let folks stay so long as they behave. Still, you shouldn't let that sheep out of your sight."

Barley looped the sheep's golden rope a few more times around his hand.

Willem smiled and thumped him on the shoulder. "No need to dampen a fine evening with worrying, though! Dinner will be ready in half an hour."

"Or it could be ready now!" Barley said. He reached his free hand into Rye's pack and pulled out the tablecloth.

"Hey!" Rye said with a quick glance at the dark corner. "No, Barley. Not here!"

"It's all right, Rye. We should share." Barley shook the tablecloth three times and spread it out on the table. A delicious feast appeared, steaming hot and ready to eat.

Willem shook his head, laughing. "That is simply amazing, but this time, don't tell everyone to come over here and help themselves. I'll serve it out to the tables."

FOUR

Late that night, after most of the other guests at the Lost Forest Inn had gone up to their rooms to bed, Barley and Rye sat by the dying fire with Willem and his family.

"Thank you for providing dinner tonight," the innkeeper said with a chuckle. "You've certainly found good fortune on your travels."

"Are you sure I can't borrow your sack?" Barley asked with a longing look at the big canvas bag hanging on the wall.

"I'm sure," the innkeeper said. "You'll find a way to manage that nix without my sack."

"I know." Barley sighed. "Dig a new well."

"We should probably all get to bed now," the innkeeper's wife said. "Willem, will you show them to their room?"

"Certainly. Follow me, please." Willem bowed with a sweep of his wing.

"One moment!" Barley said. "Willem, you said that wing is left over from a curse. Are you in love with anyone?"

THE CURSES OF LOST FOREST

"Not that I know of," Willem said.

"I have a magic petal that can break curses, but only if they have to do with true love," Barley said. He brought out his petal and showed it to Willem. "Do you want to try it?"

"Do you mean this petal could give me my hand again?" Willem raised his wing. The white feathers glowed in the dying firelight.

Willem's little sister hugged him. "I do hope it can! I've been sad every day knowing it was my mistake that gave you that wing!"

"If it wasn't for you trying to break the curse, I'd still be all goose." Willem hugged her back.

"We love you both, wing or no wing," their mother said with a fond smile.

"Try it," Barley said.

Willem reached out his wing and touched the flower petal. The feathers melted away and vanished, leaving behind an ordinary human arm.

Willem's little sister let out a happy squeal, and his mother gasped and threw her arms around them both. The innkeeper rested a hand on Willem's back and gave Barley a grateful, tearful smile. Willem curled his fingers into a fist and then opened them, watching his hand in amazement.

"Look, Rye," Barley said. He showed Rye the little pile of ash that used to be a flower petal. "I did some magic. Maybe I should be a wizard."

"How did it work?" Rye asked.

"I don't know," Barley said. "Maybe the wizard was wrong about the rules."

"That was very good of you to help Willem," Rye said softly as the innkeeper's family laughed and cried and hugged some more. "But I wonder if the time will come when you'll wish you still had that petal."

FIVE

Early the next day, before the first light of dawn, Rye checked to make sure the tablecloth was folded safely in his pack, and Barley made sure the sheep's golden rope was secure around its neck. Then, with Prince Aster riding beside them, they headed north to Humble Village. The minstrel stayed behind, as the innkeeper had been wanting a musician on his staff and the minstrel had been wanting a job. Barley and Rye promised him they'd be back to visit and hear how the songs were coming along.

By the time the sun rose, the travelers had left the Lost Forest Inn far behind, and the White River Valley spread out around them. Barley was having a hard time with the sheep. It kept skittering all over the path instead of trotting obediently at Barley's heels as it had before. Rye looked around for something that might be making the sheep nervous. High overhead, he noticed something circling against the clear blue sky, like a tiny strand of scarlet yarn with bat wings.

"Barley, that dragon is still following us," Rye said.

"Hey, dragon!" Barley shouted at the sky. "Go away! You already ate all our food!"

Either the dragon couldn't hear him, or it didn't care. It kept circling overhead as they walked, and when the travelers stopped to eat lunch, it swooped down and perched on a pile of rocks by the river.

Barley tried shaking the tablecloth and spreading it on the ground, but nothing happened. He tried shaking it and laying it on a big flat rock, but still nothing.

"We should have brought a table," Rye said.

Prince Aster shared out some dried biscuits and hard cheese that he found in his saddlebags. Rye tried not to think about the fact that the horse and its saddlebags and therefore the food inside the saddlebags had once been inside the parataxis. Barley tossed a few crumbs to the dragon, even though Prince Aster warned they'd never get rid of the little beast if he did. Rye held out a piece of cheese for the dragon, but it was too shy to come and take it from his hand.

In a hurry to return to King's Town and find his true love, Prince Aster said goodbye and galloped north as soon as he had seen Barley and Rye safely to the borders of their village. Rye almost asked to go with him, but he decided that before he went to King's Town, he wanted to see his mother and father, and have time to talk things over with Barley.

The little dragon paced along the top of the garden fence while Barley and Rye went inside their cottage to tell their parents they'd come home, then followed the Fields family all the way to the middle of the village and the boarded-up well. It perched on Molly Baker's roof as the whole village gathered around to hear what Barley and Rye had learned from the wizards.

"People of Humble Village!" Barley said. "I have consulted with the wise wizards of Wizard's Keep. Unfortunately, they were not able to give us any advice other than that we must dig another well."

The villagers cried out with disappointment.

"But my grandpapa dug this well!" Old Annie said.

"It's been in the village for generations!" another villager protested.

"You mean we have to live with that beastly nix gurgling and sloshing at us all the time?" Molly Baker's mother demanded.

Barley held his hands up until the villagers grew quiet again. "Although I was not able to learn how to remove the nix from our well, we have brought back two amazing and wonderful magical items that I promise will make up for it. This enchanted sheep sheds gold coins when you say the magic words and rub your fingers through its wool, and this magic tablecloth creates a feast when you shake it three times and spread it on a table. Our village will never want for anything again."

The villagers gasped, cheered, and clapped.

"Can it be true?"

"How wonderful!"

"Show us, Sir Barley!"

"Yes, show us, please!"

Barley asked that a table be brought. The whole village watched eagerly as he shook the tablecloth three times and laid it out on the table.

Nothing happened.

"It worked last night," Barley said. "I don't understand it!"

"Try the sheep," Rye said, trying to squash a horrible, sinking feeling that the sheep might have lost its magic too.

"*Ring tickle rit rickle!*" Barley said, and raked his fingers through the sheep's wool. The sheep let out a bleat and tried to jump away. Rye had to hold on tight to its gold rope collar. No matter how Barley raked, not a single gold coin dropped out.

The villagers stood silent for a moment. Then the tall, burly blacksmith, Nat Smith, began to laugh. "A good one, boys. Very good." Nat pressed his big hands against his leather apron as if trying to keep his laughs from bursting out of his belly. "You had me fooled. I must say I actually believed you."

Everyone else joined in, laughing along with the blacksmith.

"One of your tricks, Rye?" Jep Weaver smirked. "Very funny."

"No," Rye said. "It wasn't a trick. I promise. The magic was working last night!"

It didn't seem like anyone heard him. Still laughing, the villagers wandered away, leaving Barley and Rye standing alone by the boarded-up well.

EPISODE NINE: THE THIEF

ONE

Barley stared at the empty tablecloth in disbelief. Only last night, he'd fed every guest at the Lost Forest Inn with the magical feast it had made. But now, for some reason, the magic was gone. Not only that, but the whole village thought that he and Rye had been lying when they said they had a magic tablecloth and a magic sheep. Crushing shame squeezed his chest.

Barley's mother and father had stayed when all the other villagers had walked away. As Father set his hand on Barley's shoulder, Barley said, "It wasn't a trick, and it wasn't a lie! They really were magic!"

"I'm sure they were." Mother gave Barley a hug. "Sometimes magic wears off after a while. No matter what, we're glad to have you home."

"Barley?" Rye studied the sheep with a suspicious frown. "This sheep has been acting strange all day. Maybe it isn't our sheep."

"What do you mean?" Barley asked.

"It used to like you. But this one? It doesn't like anyone."

Barley knelt by the sheep, remembering how it had nuzzled and comforted him after the parataxis ate Rye. He reached out to pat it. The sheep jerked away from him, straining at its golden rope.

"And did our tablecloth have a stain on it?" Rye asked. "Look!"

Barley picked up the tablecloth and held it close to his face. There was a faint, yellow stain in the corner. "No, I don't think so," he said.

"Sounds like someone pulled a switch on you," said a voice Barley didn't recognize. It was a young voice, easygoing and friendly, with a King's Town accent.

Barley looked up to see a boy a little older than Rye who hadn't drifted away with the rest of the crowd. The boy's dark brown hair had an unusual gold sheen to it in the late-afternoon sun. Though Barley had never seen the boy's face, he thought he recognized the boy's blue jacket. It used to belong to Rye!

Rye gasped when he saw the boy and called out in happy disbelief, "It's you! What are you doing here? It's so marvelous to see you!"

"Oh, I just stopped by to see how you were getting along," the boy said as he came closer, hitching his pack a little higher on his back. He turned to Barley. "Hallo. You must be Sir Barley Fields. A pleasure to make your acquaintance."

Rye said, "Barley, this is the selkie who loaned me his skin so I could come rescue you from the Dragon of the

Deep." He turned to the selkie boy. "I'm so sorry. I don't remember your name."

"Fennly," the boy said.

"Glad to meet you!" Barley said. "Are you a seal?"

"Most of the time," Fennly said.

"Fennly, this is my mother and father," Rye said.

"Thank you so much for what you did to help our boys," Mother said.

"It was my pleasure." Fennly nodded to her.

Rye continued with the introductions. "And this is my village, and there on the roof is a pesky dragon that followed us all the way from Wizard's Keep, and these are obviously *not* a couple of magical items we were given in return for breaking some curses."

"Obviously," Fennly agreed.

Barley asked, "So, *did* someone take our sheep and our tablecloth and leave these in their place?"

"They must have done it while we were asleep last night. One of the other guests at the Lost Forest Inn," Rye said. He remembered the dark figures in the corner that Willem had pointed out, and the distinct feeling that they'd been very interested—too interested—in Barley's activities. "We've been robbed."

"Then we must return to the inn and find the miserable thieves who did it!" Barley put his hand on the hilt of his sword. "I'll challenge them to a duel and win our things back!"

Rye shook his head. "They'll be long gone by now."

Barley brushed his fingers over the unmagical tablecloth and sighed in frustration. He'd gone on a whole adventure to help his village, but in the end, it had done no good.

"Sorry to hear about all that," Fennly said. "But what's this about a nix in your well?"

TWO

Fennly listened, his deep brown eyes sharp, as Barley explained how the nix had appeared in the well, and how Barley and Rye had been unable to convince it to leave.

"I'll just have a little talk with him and see what's up," Fennly said. He climbed over the makeshift fence and reached for the cover of the well. "You don't mind, do you?"

"Not at all!" Barley said. "You can talk to him?"

"Sure. If he'll listen." Fennly dragged the boards aside and let them fall to the grass. The sour green smell of brackish water drifted out of the well. "Hallo down there!" Fennly called. "I'm Fennly the selkie, and I was wondering if you and I could have a little chat, one water fairy to another. What do you say?"

A gurgle came rumbling up from deep in the well. With a loud slosh, a stream of water spat up and hit Fennly in the eye.

"Ow!" Fennly stumbled back, wiping his face. "Friendly fellow, that one. Maybe I'll try again later and see if he's in a better mood."

As the sun dipped low over the Red Mountains, Barley and Rye took Fennly to the castle site. Fennly stood by the wall, smiling in admiration as he ran a hand over the white stones that blushed rose in the sunset. "This is a fine bit of work here. Coming along nicely. River stone, I'm guessing?"

"Yes," Barley said proudly. "I carried some of it up from the river myself."

"Well, that's your trouble right there," Fennly said as he stepped to the place where the hill sloped down to the riverbank. "When you took these stones from the river, you probably disturbed the nix's nest. That's the reason he moved into your well, bet you anything you like. He's just looking for a nice, deep, dark, quiet place to live. That's all. Doesn't want to have to hear all the clinking and clanking of iron tools from morning till night." Fennly pushed an iron stonecutter's chisel away with his toe as if it were something that might bite him.

"We didn't mean to disturb him," Barley said. "We didn't know he was there!"

"Here's what I'd do if I were you." Fennly rubbed his pointed chin and scanned the river. "See that lovely little watermill down the way? There's nothing a nix likes better than a spooky old millpond. Plant a few willows to shade the pond, then put all the gold you can spare deep at the bottom so's he'll have a treasure to guard. Next, set your blacksmith's shop up right next to your village well and tell the smith to hammer extra loud. When your nix is feeling good and frazzled, put a handful of gold in the well bucket and tell him that if he hops in the bucket, you'll draw him out and carry him to a nice, quiet millpond on the river."

Rye laughed and thumped Fennly on the back. "We didn't need to ask the wizards about the nix. We needed to ask you."

"Always best to consult an expert on the subject," Fennly said.

"It's a good plan, Fennly," Barley said. "We could do it if we hadn't lost our golden sheep. The gold the king gave me is nearly gone, and you can see the castle's not yet finished. I can't spare any for the nix."

"Gold is an important ingredient," Fennly said. "A nix has a weakness for the shiny yellow stuff, that's for sure."

"We've just got to get our sheep back," Barley said. "We'll go to the inn tomorrow and see if they can tell us anything."

Rye shook his head. "I don't think we'll have much chance of catching the thieves."

"Please, Rye, we have to try!" Barley said.

THREE

Fennly said he'd stay in Humble Village to direct work on the millpond while Barley and Rye went looking for their missing sheep and tablecloth. Barley spent his last few pieces of gold paying for the horses they'd borrowed and lost in the forest and buying a new pair. Early the next morning, Barley and Rye galloped south along the river until they reached the Lost Forest Inn.

"Didn't expect to see you again so soon!" Willem called cheerfully from the front yard of the inn as Barley and Rye rode up to the gate the following afternoon. Willem's bright smile faded to worry as he studied Barley's scowling face. "What's wrong?"

"We think someone stole our sheep and our tablecloth," Barley said. "They switched them for an ordinary sheep and an ordinary tablecloth, and it happened the night we were at your inn."

Rye asked, "Did you see anything suspicious that night? Do you have any idea who might have done it?"

"Nothing out of the ordinary." Willem scratched his head with fingers that used to be goose feathers. "Wait!

There is an old shepherd staying here. His sheep are in the stables. I could let you take a look and see if maybe he swapped yours for one of his."

Willem took Barley and Rye to the stables. Inside, they passed a cow with a single spiral horn in the middle of its forehead, a rooster large enough that Barley could have ridden on it, and then came to a pen with a dozen woolly white sheep crowded inside.

"Do you see it?" Willem asked.

"It could be any one of them," Rye said. "They all look alike to me."

"I'll just have to test them." Barley climbed in the pen.

"You do that," Willem said. "I'll go get my father."

In the pen, the sheep bleated and jostled each other to get as far as they could from Barley. *"Ring tickle rit rickle!"* Barley grabbed at one of the sheep, but it skipped away from him and squeezed between the others. Rye climbed in the pen and tried to hold the sheep while Barley tested them. No gold coins fell from any of the sheep they tried, but the sheep kept moving around so much, it was hard to know if they'd checked them all.

"Stop!" the innkeeper shouted from the stable door. He stood beside a tall old man in a wide-brimmed hat who was leaning on a shepherd's crook. "Your sheep isn't in that pen, boys."

"Where is it? Did you find it?" Barley asked.

"No," the innkeeper said. "But we think we know who has your things."

The old shepherd said, "I sold one of my sheep to another guest at the inn the very night you were here. He paid me a few gold coins for it, probably snatched from that pile you boys gave away."

"He left in the middle of the night, too," the innkeeper said. "No one saw him go. His room was empty in the morning."

"So he traded the sheep he bought for ours, and switched the tablecloth too, then ran off while everyone was still asleep," Rye said.

"Can you help us find him?" Barley asked the innkeeper.

"I don't know that I can," the innkeeper said. "I will tell you this. He goes by the name of Grafton Chiselwart. Curly black hair, crafty look in his eye. Been coming by now and then for about a year. Never stays more than one night, sometimes has a few friends with him, sometimes comes alone. Hasn't caused any trouble, though. Not until now."

"Do you have any idea where he would have gone?" Rye asked.

"I suspect he lives somewhere in the forest," the innkeeper said. "Other than that, I have no idea. Check the crossroads for sheep tracks. That's what I'd suggest."

FOUR

At the crossroads, Rye spotted a set of sheep hoofprints on the road that led west to the mountains. Barley and Rye followed the tracks for the rest of the afternoon. Toward evening, the shadows grew long and deep between the trees, making it harder to see the sheep's trail.

"I haven't seen any sign of our sheep for a while now." Rye crouched on the ground beside his horse, studying the dirt. "I think they went off the road. They're in the forest."

"In the forest!" Barley said. "Lost Forest is bigger than the whole Land Far Away! How are we ever going to find one man and one sheep? Do you know what we ought to do? We ought to call that fairy and see if she can help us."

"We're not calling the fairy." Rye stood up. "I say we go home. Even if we could track the sheep into the forest, we might be walking into a robber's den."

"You don't have to call the fairy," Barley said. "I will."

"Don't, Barley," Rye said. "The wizards said she was dangerous. You saw how she cursed those villages just because they forgot to say thank you."

"I'm not afraid," Barley said. "I bet she knows where our sheep is. Melinda!"

"Barley, please," Rye said.

"Melissa! Merissa? What was it, Rye? I'll keep guessing until I get it. Morinda!"

"Barley, listen to me. You've got to listen to me! If you'd listened to me at the inn, we wouldn't be in this mess!" Rye wanted to grab his brother and shake him. "It was because you showed off our sheep and our tablecloth that they got stolen."

"So it's my fault, is it?" Barley shouted back.

"Yes, in a way, it is!" Rye raised his voice to match Barley's shout.

"I just want to get our sheep and our tablecloth. Meldora!"

"Stop that!" Rye reached up, grabbed Barley around the waist, and dragged him off his horse.

"Hey! Let go!" Barley shouted as he fell on top of Rye and knocked them both to the ground. The horse flicked his ears and trotted away from the struggling boys.

Rye clamped a hand over Barley's mouth and said, "Only if you'll stop!"

Barley wrestled out of Rye's grasp and shoved him over. Rye got up and tackled him again. The two of them rolled in the dirt, Rye trying to keep Barley's mouth covered, and Barley trying to get his brother off him.

"Excuse me, boys," a trembling voice croaked sweetly from the side of the road. "Would you be kind enough to help a poor old woman?"

FIVE

Rye let go of Barley and sat up fast. An old woman in a ragged shawl and patched dress hunched under a huge bundle of sticks that was slung on her back. Rye had never seen the woman's sad, wrinkled face before, but he recognized those pale green eyes. It was the fairy, Melisma, in her old beggar woman disguise. She'd come, even though Barley hadn't said her name.

Rye shot Barley a warning glance—and saw their two horses trotting off down the road, back in the direction of the Lost Forest Inn. He scrambled to his feet to go after them, but then stopped, afraid he would offend the fairy if he left now. She had asked for help.

Barley grinned up at Rye in triumph. Rye could see Barley knew this old beggar woman was the fairy, and he was obviously glad she'd come. Too scared to speak, Rye watched Barley stand and brush himself off.

"Of course we'd be happy to help you," Barley said. "What can we do?"

"I have this heavy bundle of sticks to carry," the old woman said. "It makes my poor old back ache. Two strong young men like yourselves should have no problem lifting it, especially if you work together. Will you help me take it to my hut?"

"Be happy to," Barley said. "We'll just load it onto one of the horses, and—" Barley looked around and noticed for himself that the horses were gone. He gave Rye an angry, accusing glare. "That's the second set of horses we've lost, Rye!"

"Your horses will be fine," the old woman said. "Come help me with my bundle first, and then you can go and catch them."

The old woman slid the bundle of sticks off her back and let it clatter to the ground. When Barley and Rye went to pick it up, they could hardly move it. With a lot of grunting and struggling, they finally heaved it up on their shoulders, and together they followed the old woman into the forest.

As they went, the bundle of sticks seemed to grow heavier until they were gasping and stumbling under its weight. The sun set and the forest around them darkened. Rye began to think this might be his punishment for calling the fairy three times—to walk through an endless night with a bundle of impossibly heavy sticks on his back. He tried to take on as much of the weight as he could to make it easier for Barley, but he could still hear his brother panting with the strain.

After a long time, they came to a little moonlit clearing where a thatched hut faced an empty fire pit. "You can put the sticks down there, boys." The old woman pointed to a spot by the wall of the hut. Barley and Rye dragged themselves to the hut and dropped the sticks, then both of them collapsed on the ground in exhaustion.

The old woman said, "Now, it's been so kind of you to help me. What can I do for you in return?"

Barley sat up and asked, "Can you give us a sword for my brother, Rye?"

"What?" Rye asked. That was the last thing he had thought Barley would ask for. What about the sheep and the tablecloth? Or the nix in the well? Or even just finding their horses again?

The old woman seemed surprised too. "A sword?" she asked.

"A nice one," Barley said. "Maybe a little bit magic? Just a little. If it isn't too much trouble."

"If you'll look in my hut, you will find two swords," the old woman said. "One for each of you. The blades will stay bright so long as you are both safe and well, but if your sword should ever rust, you will know your brother is in peril and needs your aid."

Rye stood up as Barley disappeared into the dark opening of the hut. "Thank you," Rye said to the old woman. He couldn't help feeling excited at the thought of having his own sword, especially a magical one that would tell him when Barley was in trouble. So long as it was bright, he would never need to worry. If Rye made sure to be extra polite and grateful, and didn't offend the fairy in any way, maybe they could get out of this mess and go home.

The old woman only smiled. It wasn't a very nice smile, either.

Barley came out of the hut, beaming, carrying a sword in each hand. He gave one to Rye, then stepped back and slashed his new sword through the air a couple of times. The blade gleamed bright in the moonlight. "These are nice! Worth carrying a bundle of sticks made out of lead for half the night, wouldn't you say, Rye?"

Rye was about to say the gift was worth far more than that, but the old woman spoke first. "Ungrateful boy!" She pointed a crooked finger at Barley. "I have given you a magnificent gift, and all you can think is to complain about the small task I asked of you."

"Barley, say thank you!" Rye said.

It was too late. Barley's gold curls, his smiling face, and the hand that gripped the sword's hilt had all turned the dull, dark gray of lead. His figure stood silent and un-moving, swallowing the moonlight like a shadow.

"Oh, look!" the old woman pointed to Rye's sword and giggled. "It works!"

Rye glanced down to see the sword in his hand covered with rust.

EPISODE TEN: MELISMA'S CURSE

.

ONE

Rye dropped the rusted sword like it was poison. Ice-cold chills ran up his arms, and his stomach curled into a knot so tight, it stole his breath. "Turn him back!" he panted.

The old woman was gone. Her hunched form had vanished, along with the empty fire pit, the hut—even the bundle of sticks. Rye stood alone in a small clearing of a moonlit forest with nothing but a rusty sword and a lead statue of his brother.

"Turn him back!" Rye howled, flinging the sound from the empty ache in his heart. The cry rang through the quiet night. His chest swelled with the desire to hurt, to strike back. There was nothing for him to fight. His anger slowly faded, leaving sick despair behind. "Turn him back," Rye whispered to Barley's unmoving face. The lead mouth's frozen lips smiled at the moon-touched blade in Barley's lead hand.

The fairy had cursed Barley to get back at Rye. All the times Rye called her, he never asked for anything for himself, not once. He'd only called her to help other people, and most of them were people she had cursed herself. For trying to help others, this was his reward. His brother turned to lead.

"Melisma!" Rye roared her name into the night sky.

Brilliant white light filled the clearing. Wind whipped the branches in the trees. "I told you never to call me again!" the fairy shrieked as she appeared at the center of the whirling storm, her beautiful face ugly with rage. Vast wings made of cloud and lightning filled the sky behind her.

Rye wanted to shout that she should have known he'd call her after what she'd done to his brother, but he didn't. She had probably wanted him to call her so she could find a way to curse him too. He was going to play this carefully, so carefully she'd never have the chance. She was a curse herself. Cursed . . .

"*You've* been cursed!" Rye said, so shocked by the realization, it was out of his mouth before he had time to think what she might do to him if he knew it. "You have to come when anyone calls your name, and you have to . . ."

The fairy screamed in fury. Wind tore branches from the trees and flung them, crashing, into the clearing. Some landed inches from Rye, but not one touched him.

"You have to do what you're asked!" Rye shouted over the storm.

Everything in the clearing grew still. The light faded to a soft, white glow around the fairy. Her wings shrank to silvered gossamer. The wary resignation in her pale green eyes told Rye that what he had guessed was true.

"Ask me to restore your brother," the fairy said, her voice bitter with defeat. "Keep my secret, and I'll never trouble you again."

Rye shook his head. He wanted very much to do as the fairy said, to have her turn Barley back that instant, but if he did, the fairy would go on cursing people. He understood now. She did it to frighten them so no one would dare call her name and ask her a favor. "I want to know the story. Tell me how you were cursed."

The fairy's eyes widened in horror. "No! Ask me anything else! Please!"

When you know the true story, the solution will be clear.

"Tell me the story," Rye said. "If I know the story, maybe I can help you break your curse."

"Mortal! Human worm! Do you think I haven't tried to break this curse? I've tried everything in my power, and nothing, nothing has worked!"

"Tell me the story," Rye said.

The fairy stared back at him in disbelief, as if she couldn't understand why he would ask such a thing. Then she bowed her head. Her dark hair slid like a curtain to cover her face. She slowly reached out her hand, as if some force against her will made her do it.

"Come. I will show you."

TWO

Rye hesitated, afraid to touch the fairy's outstretched hand. She waited with her face turned to the ground. Rye closed his hand around her fingers. They were cool and hard, more like candle wax than human flesh. He shuddered, wondering if what he saw and touched was her true form or only another illusion.

The trees around them grew taller, older, filling the sky with their canopies and blocking all but a few bright shafts of moonlight. Strange calls from insects, frogs, and night birds Rye couldn't name filled the air. A heavy, sweet scent of flowers mixed with dewy grass and rich earth. Even in the darkness of night, this forest thrummed with life.

Except for in the dead place. Directly in front of them, a blackness deeper than the night consumed the trees. The sun swept into the sky, moving impossibly fast. In the darkness ahead of them, the trees stayed black, wrapped in an ever-present night. Leaves fell from skeleton branches. The living night crept forward, shriveling the grass and turning the flowers to dust. Silence and a bitter stench of decay advanced over the forest. Rye backed away one step.

The scene changed. Trees stretched and became tall stone pillars that held up a stone ceiling. A vast underground hall took shape, hung with tapestries and garnished with gold. Fairies flocked the hall, wings gleaming blue in the coldfire torches, jewels flashing on their clothes and in their hair. Together they shouted a wild, fierce battle cry. Together they rushed out of their hall, running or flying.

Rye and Melisma went with them, though to Rye it seemed he never moved at all. From high over the trees, he stood and watched the fairies fight the dead darkness consuming their forest. They burned it with coldfire. They washed it with clear rain and pure running water. They raised living trees and plants from the earth where the ground had gone bare. The darkness pushed forward, consuming all their efforts. Fairies with limbs touched by the black rot were carried back to their underground home in the arms of their friends, who tended to them as they sickened and crumbled away.

Out in the forest, in the middle of the battle, a fairy woman with a crown and a staff chose seven of her subjects and gave them orders Rye couldn't hear. The seven fairies flew out of sight, and then, after a time, each returned with an army of magical creatures. Dragons burned the darkness with their breath. Trolls, dwarves, and giants dug a great trench between the darkness and the living forest. Wizards filled the trench with healing waters. Witches put protective spells over the trees. Unicorns healed the wounded. They all fought together, side by side with the fairies, and gradually, the darkness fell back. Rye cheered along with the fairies and their allies when the last of the darkness vanished and the forest was green again. It had taken all of them, working together, to win the war.

All except for one. One young fairy girl had stayed in the underground halls, never going out to fight, never tending the wounded and dying. Rye watched, indignant, as she amused herself with her harp and her books while others faced danger and fought to protect her home.

When the war ended, the fairy queen called this fairy to appear before her.

"Why did you not answer the summons to battle when my realm was threatened?" the fairy queen demanded.

"I am only one," the fairy answered, and when she spoke, Rye realized it was Melisma. She was the fairy who hadn't fought in the war. He turned to see that beside him, Melisma had angry tears on her face as she watched her younger self. "I am small and weak. What difference did it make that I did not fight?"

"What difference? If you had helped us with your small strength, this much of the forest would never have been touched by the darkness." The fairy queen gestured with her staff, and a vision appeared of a meadow, bright with wildflowers and ringed with ancient trees. The trees crumbled to black and the meadow turned bare.

As the vision faded, the queen declared, "Because you would not help us in our time of need, you are banished to Lost Forest. Furthermore, you are cursed that you must go and help any creature in that forest who calls your name until you have learned your lesson!"

THREE

The fairy hall vanished. Rye and Melisma stood in Lost Forest, among slender trees, under a sky turning the purple-gray of dawn. Seeing Barley in the clearing still turned to lead struck Rye like a stab to his heart. He lurched forward, gasping at the pain, and pulled his hand away from Melisma's grasp. As the ache subsided enough that he could breathe and speak, he knew what needed to be done. He knew how to break the fairy's curse, but it wasn't anything he could do. It was up to the fairy. He wasn't sure he could make her understand.

"Do you know what you have to do?" Rye asked. His breath fogged in the cold.

"To break my curse? Learn my lesson, I suppose. What do they want me to learn? I've been forced to help more of you worthless mortals than I can count! It does me no good. I'm still cursed. I'm sick of it. You're all so *ungrateful!*"

"The curse forces you to help others, but you haven't learned to be helpful," Rye said. "If you're really being helpful, you don't care whether you're doing only a little good or a lot. You don't ask for anything in return. Not even thanks. If you're really being helpful, you don't even have to be asked to help. Have you ever helped someone without being asked?"

For a long time, Melisma said nothing. Birds called to each other through the trees, and a single yellow leaf twirled down and landed on Barley's lead shoulder. As the light grew stronger, Rye noticed dust on Barley's face. A frosted layer of dead leaves lay scattered over the rusted sword on the ground. All the breath squeezed out of him. How long had it taken the fairy to show him her story?

"I have done what you asked," Melisma said. "I owe you nothing."

Rye didn't dare say a word.

Melisma stepped over a fallen branch that was all dried up and beginning to decay, as if it had lain there for months instead of falling only last night. She reached for Barley's lead curls. The instant she touched him, color washed over him like he'd stepped out of a shadow and into the sunlight. Barley gave a small squeak of terror and ducked away from the fairy, then looked around in confusion.

"It's morning already? And . . ." Barley coughed and brushed at his jacket. "I'm all cobwebs and dust! Rye, what happened?"

The only answer Rye gave was to grab his brother in a tight hug. "Thank you," Rye said, and this time, he wasn't just saying it to avoid offending the fairy. This time he really meant it.

FOUR

"No, really, what happened?" Barley asked as he hugged Rye back.

Rye let out a short laugh. "She turned you to lead, and I didn't ask her to turn you back."

"You didn't?" Barley asked. "I'm confused. Why is it so cold, and . . . why is there moss growing on my boots?"

"Did it work?" Rye asked the fairy as he let go of Barley. "Is your curse broken?"

"I'm not sure," the fairy said. "We'll have to test it. I'll go away, and you try calling me."

Rye nodded.

"I really don't understand what's going on," Barley said, frowning at all the dead, broken branches that littered the clearing. "Where's your sword, Rye? Oh, there it is. Why is it on the ground?"

The fairy vanished in a whisper of soft chimes.

"I got turned to lead?" Barley asked, noticing how the treetops blazed with autumn color as the first rays of morning touched their tops. Only yesterday afternoon, the leaves had been spring green. Or had that been only yesterday? Prickles colder than the frosty morning crawled along his back. "For how long?"

Rye held up his hand and shook his head. Barley wasn't sure if that meant he didn't know, or if it meant he wanted Barley to be quiet.

"Melisma," Rye said.

Chimes tinkled, and the fairy appeared with her arms crossed. She scowled and tapped her foot. "Yes?"

"It didn't work?" Rye asked, his eyes wide with worry. "Oh, no! I was sure that would do it. Here—let me think. There's got to be something else we could try."

The fairy's fierce expression melted into giggles. "It worked. I was only teasing. I came because I wanted to."

"You did?" Rye asked, still tense and afraid. Barley blinked, surprised to hear the fairy laugh. She'd always seemed so grumpy before.

"Yes," the fairy said. "I wanted to tell you to go home. Your sheep and your tablecloth are there already."

"Thank you!" Barley said, so happy to hear it that he almost forgot to be upset by finding himself in an autumn forest at dawn when the last thing he knew, it had been springtime and the middle of the night. "Thank you very much!"

The fairy dropped into a low curtsy while fluttering her wings elegantly, and then vanished before she'd straightened up.

Barley narrowed his eyes at Rye. "She turned me to lead, and you *didn't* ask her to turn me back?"

Rye picked up his sword from the ground and wiped the bright metal blade clean on his sleeve. "I'll tell you the story as we walk."

FIVE

Instead of wasting time trying to find the road, Barley and Rye struck their own path through the forest, keeping the morning sun ahead and to their right. Near noon, they came out of the trees on the edge of a wide, autumn-gold grassland with a distant silver ribbon twining through it— the White River.

That night, on the river's bank, they roasted and ate the fish they'd caught with the hook and line Rye always carried in his pocket, and then huddled for warmth in a dry, sandy hollow under the overhanging roots of a tree.

"What if we haven't been gone only one summer?" Barley asked. "What if it's been seven years, or a hundred? What if everyone's forgotten us?"

Rye stared at the patch of starry night sky above the trees on the far side of the river, his face dim in the last red light of their campfire. "We'll find out tomorrow." He sounded worried too.

"I can't believe that when the fairy offered to turn me back the first time, you decided to help her break her curse instead." Barley thought that if it had been Rye in trouble, he would have helped him first and then taken care of the fairy after.

"She would have gone on cursing people if I didn't." Rye was not being as apologetic as Barley would have liked. "She was hurting others because she needed help."

"I needed help," Barley said. "I was a lead statue all summer long."

"Didn't do you any harm, did it?" Rye sounded a little irritated. He yawned and rolled over, putting his back to Barley.

"Maybe it did, if it's been a hundred years." Barley pulled the blue pebble Janet Grover had given him out of his pocket, rubbed it with his thumb, then tucked it away again.

Six

Barley and Rye hadn't gone far the next morning before they saw a distant white castle gleaming like a diamond beside the banks of the river. "Is that my castle?" Barley asked. "It's bigger! Is it finished? Where did they get the gold to do it?"

"From the sheep, I suppose," Rye said. He squinted into the shimmering haze over the grasslands, trying to count the towers. He couldn't tell if there were six or seven. At any rate, it was more than Barley had planned to build.

"How did they know the magic words?" Barley asked.

"They were paying attention when we tried to show them with the wrong sheep?" Rye suggested. He doubted it was true. Something wasn't right.

As they came closer, they noticed that not only was the castle bigger, but the village was bigger too. Much bigger. Houses and huts had sprung up all around the castle. So many people, some in regular work clothes and others in uniform like soldiers or guards, moved around between the buildings. Shabby wooden shacks stood in rows on the very same field where Barley and Rye had been harvesting the day they'd first met Wizard Thornberry. The castle itself had walls as high as three village huts stacked on top of each other, and seven round towers of different sizes. Wanting to find out if their family and friends still lived in Humble Village, but also afraid to learn that they didn't, Barley and Rye hurried along the road.

"Barley!" a girl's anxious voice called out from a thicket of trees beside the river.

Rye turned to see Janet Grover watching them from up in one of the trees. He smiled with relief. If Janet was there, the rest of the villagers he knew were probably around too.

"Janet!" Barley said. "Oh, I'm so glad you're not a hundred years old!"

"Get off the road! They're watching for you!" Janet said, nearly in tears. She scrambled down through the branches and then jumped the rest of the way to the ground.

"What's the matter?" Rye asked as he and Barley darted into the shade of the thicket. "Who's watching for us?"

"The Lord of Lost Castle!" Janet said, leading them deeper into the trees. "He came a week after you went away, with all his brigands, plus dozens more, and he took over the village and your castle, and he had a sheep with him!"

"A sheep?" Barley asked. "Our magic sheep?"

"We're not sure. No one has ever seen him use it, but he seems to have all the gold he could possibly want. And no one brings food into the castle, but he and his men and all his soldiers feast every night. His army gets bigger every day. They say he plans to march on King Hugric and conquer the Land Far Away before the first snows."

THE CURSES OF LOST FOREST

"That fairy!" Rye said, gritting his teeth. "Our sheep and our tablecloth are already here, true enough, but she left out a few important details."

Barley plopped down on a rock. "What are we going to do?"

"I don't know, but you've got to be careful," Janet said. "Lord Chiselwart—that's what he calls himself now—he's got all his men looking for you. He'll put you in his dungeon if he catches you. I've been watching the road for you every day to warn you in case you came back."

"Chiselwart," Rye said. "That's what the innkeeper said." He shook his head and paced the narrow space between the trees. "That man the innkeeper described—I never even thought he might be the Lord of Lost Castle. I bet that was him and his brigands watching us from the corner of the inn that night we were there."

"Are our mother and father all right?" Barley asked.

Janet said, "Yes, everyone in the village is all right, but we have to work night and day to make weapons for the army. No one is allowed out of the village. Old Chiselface is afraid someone will go and warn King Hugric. I found a way to sneak in and out so I could watch for you." She beamed at Barley. "I'm so glad you're home! After all this time, we didn't know if you were ever coming back!"

"We had some trouble with a fairy," Barley said.

"That selkie boy went looking for you after Chiselwart came, but we never saw him again either," Janet said.

"He wouldn't have been able to find us," Barley said.

"Not unless he was looking for a lead statue of me standing in the middle of the forest."

Janet gave Barley a puzzled frown.

"Do you think the innkeeper would let us borrow his sack for this?" Rye asked. "We could go back to the inn and ask."

"We just got home!" Barley said. "I don't want to leave again. Not until we've set things right."

"How are we going to do that on our own?" Rye asked. "We can't fight an entire army."

"No, we can't," Barley said. "And the only reason this Chiselwart *has* an army is because of our sheep and our tablecloth. I can't believe he stole them from us!"

Rye felt the beginnings of an idea come into his head. He asked Janet, "Can you get us close to the castle?"

"Do you have a plan, Rye?" Barley asked.

Rye nodded. "We're going to steal our sheep and our tablecloth back."

Episode Eleven: The Storming of Humble Castle

ONE

Janet led Barley and Rye along the riverbed toward Humble Village. They kept to the groves and stands of rushes, crept through the brambles, and hid under the bank. At last they came, torn, scratched, and muddy, to the place where the river flowed closest by the castle.

Barley grumbled, "If I'd known that I'd have to break into my own castle, I would have had the workmen dig a secret tunnel to the river. You'd have to go underwater to get to the opening, and it would come out right about here, and the other end of it would have a trap door that led right up into the main sleeping chambers."

Rye gave Barley a look of open admiration. "Please tell me you've already done this," he said, his voice breathless with hope.

"No!" Barley said, indignant. "It didn't cross my mind until this very moment."

Rye slouched against the sandy riverbank. "We'll get to work on it once we've taken the castle back." He thumped his hand on Barley's shoulder.

"I'll put secret passages all over the castle," Barley said. "It'll have so many secret passages, I won't ever have to use the halls."

They settled in the cold, damp gravel to wait until nightfall, when it would be easier to creep close to the castle walls unseen. Barley watched the sky, wishing for the clouds to grow thicker so they'd hide the moon and give them more cover once it got dark.

A shout came from the direction of the castle. Loud, angry voices followed, along with a trilling screech that sounded like . . .

"Is that the dragon?" Barley asked.

"I'll go look," Rye said. He left his sword on a rock, climbed the bank, and stayed low in the tall grass as he crawled up the hill. After a minute, he gestured for Barley to come up beside him.

With his new sword in his hand, and after checking that his old one was secure at his belt, Barley climbed until he could see the top of the nearest castle tower. A thin stream of smoke rose from smoldering shingles near a shabby nest perched on top of a window gable. Hovering over the nest, the little red dragon that had followed them from Wizard's Keep screeched and snapped at a soldier who leaned out the window. The soldier poked at the nest with his spear. Other soldiers on the parapets next to the tower watched, shouting encouragement to their comrade.

"Now's our chance!" Barley said. "Let's break in while they're all busy with the dragon."

Rye held up his hand and shook his head. Barley wasn't sure if that meant *not yet* or *not ever*. He frowned at Rye. Why couldn't he see that this was a perfect opportunity? The time to go was right now.

The dragon hissed and spat a thin stream of fire at the soldier. The man yelped, dropped his spear, and used his hands to beat the flames out of his beard. After he disappeared inside the window, another soldier took his place, this one bolder, who climbed onto the windowsill and tried to grab the nest. The dragon swooped at him, raking his helmet with its claws. The soldier almost fell, but another soldier at the window grabbed his legs and held him steady. Arrows began to arc over the tower, shot by bowmen on the parapets.

"I wish they'd leave it alone," Janet said. She had climbed up to watch too. "Poor thing."

The dragon gave one last furious screech and picked up the nest in its claws. As the nest lifted from the roof, something small and copper-colored tumbled out and fell toward the ground. Janet gasped when it fell. The dragon didn't seem to notice. It flapped away, trilling angrily and hauling the nest along. One tiny red head and one tiny yellow head peeked over the rim of the nest before the dragon flew away out of sight.

"It was a mother dragon!" Barley whispered in surprise.

"Stay here," Rye said. "I'll be right back."

"Stay here?" Barley asked, but Rye had already scrambled higher up the side of the hill.

On top of the castle wall, the soldiers cheered and shouted rude things at the dragon as it flew away. One soldier with a bucket of water reached out of the window and tried to douse the smoking tower roof. He kept throwing the water in the wrong direction and soaking either himself or someone standing on the parapet below. None of the soldiers were watching the hillside.

"Stay here," Barley said to Janet. "We're going in now."

Barley scrambled up the side of the hill, dashed to the castle wall, and pressed his back against the stones. Beside him, Rye crouched near the wall, cupping something in his hands. A tiny baby dragon, its head as big as the rest of its body, curled motionless in Rye's palm. Rye glanced up at the tower overhead as if measuring the distance the baby dragon had fallen. He gave Barley a sad look.

Barley nodded to let Rye know he felt bad for the baby dragon too. From where Barley stood, he could see the soldier leaning from the window, trying to put the fire out. If that soldier looked down, they'd be seen. They had to move before they got caught.

"Excuse me!"

Barley tried not to gasp when he heard Janet's voice. She stood on the hillside on the far side of the tower, out in the open where all the soldiers could see her! Of course, if the soldiers were all looking at her, they wouldn't see Barley and Rye by the castle wall.

"Excuse me!" Janet said again, louder. "Did you know your tower is on fire?"

"Of course we do, you stupid girl!" All the soldiers on the parapet stared down at Janet. "Go back to the village! Aren't you supposed to be working?"

Barley motioned for Rye to follow him along the wall. Rye glanced at the river, at Janet, at the soldiers on the wall, as if trying to judge whether they could make it back down the hill without being seen. Barley shook his head. He did not want to go back to hiding by the river, not after they'd made it this far.

Rye nodded reluctantly and indicated with a little tip of his head for Barley to keep moving along the wall. Barley crept toward the next tower with Rye moving softly behind him. If they could make it around the base of the next tower, they'd be out of sight from the soldiers. Barley thought that if Janet kept the soldiers distracted long enough, he might be able to climb up in the corner where the tower joined the castle wall and get onto the parapets without being seen.

"You're going to want to put that fire out, you know!" Janet said.

"Get out of here! No one is allowed near the castle!"

"I just thought someone ought to warn you," Janet said. "About the fire."

Barley reached the tower, checked to make sure all the soldiers were still focused on Janet, then dashed around the tower's base. On the far side of the tower, he almost ran into three men coming from the other direction.

"Well, hello!" One of them showed his crooked teeth in a nasty smile. Barley jerked backward, recognizing the very same three brigands who had captured Rye and taken him to Lost Castle. For a moment, Barley felt like the same frightened little boy who had hidden under a blackberry bush while his brother was taken away.

"We've been wondering when you'd show up," said one of the other brigands. He looked toward the top of the castle wall and shouted, "Guards! Over here!"

Barley stood tall and raised his sword. They weren't going to take either of them this time! "Rye, run for the river!" Barley shouted.

The three men drew their own swords and backed away. "That's not the sword he had last time," one of them said. "Is it?"

"Barley, stand down," Rye said in a terrified voice.

Barley's hand trembled when he saw tiny spots of rust appear along his sword's blade. He backed protectively toward Rye.

"Don't move!" shouted a voice from overhead. Barley looked up at the parapets to see dozens of arrows and spears pointed in their direction.

Another soldier on the wall shouted at Janet, "Don't you move either! Stay right where you are, all of you, or we'll shoot!"

"Drop the sword," one of the brigands growled.

Barley let his sword fall to the ground and held his hands up in surrender. Sneaking into his own castle had gone about as badly as could possibly be expected.

TWO

"To be honest, I was worried about what might happen when you came back." Grafton Chiselwart wiped the corner of his moustache with a napkin. His greasy black curls had grown wilder, the mean look in his small, dark eyes had grown fiercer, and his hands now gleamed with jeweled rings. Other than that, he was the very same man Barley had fought with the magic sword and chased out of Lost Castle. "You boys have quite a reputation, vanquishing mighty sea dragons and all. I'm relieved to see that the tales of your cunning and ability have all been greatly exaggerated."

The brigands around the room laughed. Their chief sat before a magnificent feast with a familiar plain linen tablecloth spread underneath it. Near his chair, a sad-looking sheep knelt on the floor of a wooden crate.

"You stole our sheep!" Barley shouted, straining forward against the two brigands who held him by the arms. "And our tablecloth! And my castle!"

"Mmmm." Lord Chiselwart nodded and smiled as if Barley had given him a compliment. He wiggled his fingers so that his rings clicked together. "Yes, thank you. I may be the only robber chief alive who has managed to steal not one, but two castles. No reason to stop there, eh, boys?"

The brigands shouted out a cheer and shook their fists in the air. They had all gathered in the main hall and seemed eager to see what their master might do to Sir Barley Fields, the young knight who had humiliated them at the Battle of Lost Castle. Their clothes were finer now, and they looked more well fed, but their hair and beards were still shaggy and their faces still grimy.

Rye, who was being held by another pair of robbers, kept turning his eyes around the room as if searching for something, though Barley couldn't imagine what. Barley was most worried about Janet Grover, who looked so tiny next to all of Lord Chiselwart's brigands. She stared, wide-eyed and speechless with terror, seeming to shrink even smaller at the brigands' shouts.

Lord Chiselwart served himself another slice of ham. "Now that I have all the food and money I could possibly want, there's no limit to the number of men I can command. I think it shows a serious lack of imagination on your part that you didn't immediately come to the same conclusion. Trust me, I'll put all of this to better use than you ever would." He showed his teeth in a smug grin as he pointed his serving fork at the tablecloth, then the sheep, and then at Barley.

"You think our sheep and our tablecloth will give you an advantage in war?" Rye asked, his voice sharp and scornful.

At Lord Chiselwart's feet lay the magic sword Barley had been given by the fairy, along with his knight's sword and a small knife that Janet had been carrying. When Rye spoke, more rust spots bloomed on the magic sword's blade.

Barley shot Rye a warning glance, but Rye didn't see him. Rye was too busy glaring at Lord Chiselwart.

"Of course they will," Lord Chiselwart said. "They already have."

Rye said, "There's a village in the Lost Forest where everyone has a tablecloth like that one, and another village where there's an entire flock of sheep like the one in that crate. If you try to conquer the Emerald Realms using these magic things, others with an even greater advantage will come against you and defeat you."

"Rye!" Barley said, shocked. What was he trying to do? Even Barley could see it wasn't a good idea to tell Lord Chiselwart where they'd gotten the sheep and the tablecloth.

Lord Chiselwart stopped smiling. "If what you say is true, these villages must be equally lacking in imagination. If I move against them now, take them and their magical things, they will be no threat to me."

The brigands muttered their approval.

"No!" Rye said. He looked startled. "That's not . . . you can't! You'll never find them."

"Yes, I will." Lord Chiselwart stood up. "You will lead me there."

Rye shook his head. He seemed horrified by what he'd done.

The brigands around the room laughed and slapped each other on the back as Lord Chiselwart stepped to where his men held Rye. "You will lead me and my army there. No tricks and no trouble from either of you, or you and your brother both die. Is that understood?"

THREE

When Barley had included a dungeon in the plans for his castle, he never thought he'd actually use it. He only put one in because he thought a proper castle really ought to have a dungeon. He certainly wouldn't have guessed that on the first night he spent in his own castle, he'd be sleeping in one of the dungeon cells.

"Barley?" Rye called softly from the next cell over. "The baby dragon's still alive. I got it to drink some water."

"Is it?" Janet asked in a teary voice from another cell across the room. "I'm so glad."

"It's hurt badly, though," Rye said. "I wish I had some way to set this wing."

Barley rolled over on the hard wooden bench and stared at the tiny window grate high in the cell wall. If Rye hadn't gone and picked up that baby dragon, they might be hiding in the riverbed, waiting for the perfect chance to break into the castle. Of course, if Barley hadn't been so eager to show Willem what his magic sheep could do, Barley might be sleeping upstairs in his own castle bedroom instead of on a cold, hard bench in the dungeon.

"Janet?" Rye asked. "Will you take care of it? When they come to get us tomorrow, I'll see if I can pass it to you. I don't think I should take it with me. It needs to lie still and rest."

"Yes, I'll take care of it," Janet said.

On the far side of the dungeon door, the guards burst out hooting and laughing over some unexpected turn in their game of dice. Barley could smell the good food they were enjoying, thanks to the magic tablecloth Lord Chiselwart had stolen. As for Barley, he hadn't touched the bowl of tasteless porridge with not quite enough salt that the guards had given him for his supper.

"Rye, we can't let them attack those villages in the Lost Forest," Barley said. "Not after the villagers were so kind to us!"

"I know," Rye said.

"What do we do? We could refuse to show Lord Chiselwart where they are. I mean, we'd be dead, but the villages would be safe."

"I'm not sure he'd stop at killing us if we don't do as he says." Rye's voice sounded empty, as if he'd completely given up. "Our whole village—everyone is in danger."

Janet sniffled. "I thought everything would turn out right as soon as you two came back."

"I'm sorry, Janet," Barley said. "Please don't cry."

"I'm trying not to," Janet sobbed.

"Do you think that fairy might help us?" Barley asked, desperate for something they could do. He hated to see the small shadow that was Janet curled up against the bars of her cell, shaking with misery.

"I think that fairy knew she was sending us into a trap," Rye said, his voice bitter. "Do you really want her help?"

"Then what are we going to do?" Barley asked.

Rye didn't answer.

FOUR

The next morning, Grafton Chiselwart set out on his campaign against the villages of Crystal Springs and Appledale. He rode at the head of five hundred men, leaving his band of brigands and the rest of his army to watch over his castle. Down in the dungeon, Janet Grover, who now had Rye's baby dragon, was to be imprisoned until Lord Chiselwart's successful return.

Barley hadn't seen where the tablecloth was, but the sheep trotted along next to him. Both Barley and the sheep had been roped by the neck to one of the supply carts. The sheep, who didn't know any better, skipped along happily. It kept giving Barley friendly bumps with its round woolly head. It must have been glad to be out of that crate and with someone it liked. Barley would have given it a grateful pat in return except that his hands were tied behind his back.

Up at the front of the line, Rye walked alongside Lord Chiselwart's horse, his hands tied behind his back and the rope around his neck tied to Lord Chiselwart's saddle horn. Barley could tell by the way Rye stumbled along with his shoulders drooping and his head down, that he still hadn't come up with a plan.

As they passed through Humble Village, Barley heard his mother calling his name. He turned to see her dart into the column of soldiers, trying to reach him. The soldiers held her back.

"Mother!" Barley called to her, his heart torn by how sad and worn she looked.

"Quiet!" One of the guards who had been assigned to watch Barley gave him a shove. "You're not allowed to speak!"

Barley's father came running and pulled Barley's sobbing mother away from the soldiers. Barley's mother and father stood together with their arms around each other, watching silently as the army marched away.

Toward the end of a long, miserable, weary day of walking, Barley had an idea. If they went by the Lost Forest Inn, Willem and his family would see what was happening and figure out some way to help them. He could just imagine the innkeeper coming out in the front yard with his magic sack and telling Lord Chiselwart to pop into it. Maybe the innkeeper would tell the whole army to pop into the sack. Barley wasn't sure how it worked. Could the innkeeper fit a whole army in that sack, or could he only keep one thing at a time in it?

Barley never found out. Long before they reached the Lost Forest Inn, Lord Chiselwart turned his army off the road and marched west. They camped on the plains that night. Barley noticed that Lord Chiselwart used the tablecloth, but didn't let any of his soldiers see him doing it. He went into a tent, then after a while came out and ordered a few of his men to hand around the food. Barley thought the soldiers probably didn't know about the sheep, either. The soldiers all seemed to think Lord Chiselwart was a wealthy magician who could make food appear out of nowhere, and they liked bragging to each other about what they were going to do with all the gold he'd promised to pay them. Barley thought about telling them where the food and gold really came from, but he couldn't see exactly how that would help him and Rye escape. Letting other people know about the sheep and the tablecloth had gotten him in a lot of trouble last time. Besides that, Lord Chiselwart had ordered the soldiers not to let Barley speak.

As he tried to fall asleep that night, huddled under the cart with the sheep, Barley wondered about Rye. He wondered if Rye's neck was sore and raw from having a rope around it all day. He wondered if Rye regretted telling Lord Chiselwart where the magic sheep and the magic tablecloth had come from. He especially wondered what Rye was going to do tomorrow.

Episode Twelve: One Last Curse

ONE

The next day, as far as Barley could tell, Rye did very little except walk. The army marched south into the forest, then east until they came to the river road, as if Grafton Chiselwart had decided to go a half-day's journey out of his way in order to avoid the Lost Forest Inn. If it had been Rye's plan to rely on help from the innkeeper, that hope was gone.

Barley thought Rye might try to lead Lord Chiselwart's army to get lost in the forest, like they had been on their journey to Wizard's Keep. But when they came to the place where the road turned west into the forest, they didn't follow it. Rye must have told Lord Chiselwart to keep to the river. The army marched along the riverbank for the rest of the day, though the lack of a road made their travel slow. In some places, the army had to stop and cut down trees to let the carts through. That night, as exhausted as he was, Barley couldn't sleep. His neck and wrists stung from the rope that had been scraping at them all day. Worse, he knew that tomorrow Lord Chiselwart's army would reach the village of Crystal Springs.

Around noon the next day, the army came to a halt. At first, Barley thought they'd stopped to cut their way through again, but then he saw the ferryman's platform down the river. The ferryman pushed his pole into the water and drew it out, inching the platform toward the bank. Barley gasped, and then he grinned. Now here was an opportunity! He wondered if Rye had been thinking this all along. It could be the reason Rye had told Lord Chiselwart about Crystal Springs and Appledale. Now that they were here, there had to be some way to get Lord Chiselwart to take that pole from the ferryman. Barley was sure Rye would figure it out, whatever it was.

A group of soldiers came jogging from the front of the line to where Barley stood. One of them untied the sheep's rope from the cart, and another one took Barley's rope. "Up to the front with you," said the soldier with Barley's rope. "Quickly now."

Barley half ran and half stumbled to keep up with the soldiers who had been sent to fetch him. The sheep, who was far more exhausted than it had been on the first day, bleated in protest, but broke into a shambling trot. When they reached the front of the army, the ferryman had almost reached the shore.

From high on his horse, Lord Chiselwart scowled suspiciously down at the ferry platform, at the ferryman, and especially at Rye. It had been over two days since Barley had seen Rye up close, and he looked terrible. Dark circles ringed his eyes, and yellow crust scabbed the sores from the rope on his neck.

"I can only take a few across at a time," the ferryman said in his weary voice, not showing any sign that he recognized Barley or Rye. He must have recognized them, Barley thought. He must know they needed his help. He was only pretending he didn't remember them so Lord Chiselwart wouldn't be even more suspicious.

"Hand me that sheep," Lord Chiselwart ordered. "I'll go first, with this one." He nodded his head at Rye. "Hold the other one here until we're all across, and if there's any trouble at all, you're to twist that rope and strangle him dead, then throw him in the river, do you understand?"

Barley felt the soldier behind him grip the rope tight behind the back of his neck. His whole body went stiff with pain and fright. Desperate, he looked to Rye for help. Rye glanced at the ferryman, then at Barley, his face pale and his eyes feverish with worry. If Rye had been planning something, it didn't look like his plan included this.

Lord Chiselwart urged his horse onto the ferry platform. "Wait." He glared back over his shoulder at Barley. His eyes narrowed. The corner of his mouth twitched up in a smirk. "I'll take the little one with me instead."

Two

Barley breathed out as the rope loosened. Everything seemed unreal, as if he were floating. His feet stumbled onto the ferry platform, but he was too stunned to feel them. A soldier towed him forward by the arm and handed the end of Barley's rope to Lord Chiselwart. Barley saw Rye's shoulders sag with relief. Rye gave Barley a nod, and was that a wink? What did that mean? Barley shook his head, confused. He watched as Rye was led onto the shore and turned to face the river.

Rye's jaw tightened and his breath quickened as the soldier behind him got a firm grip on the rope at Rye's neck. Even so, Rye gave Barley a small, encouraging smile. For an instant, Barley thought he saw the spark of mischief that meant Rye had a trick in mind, but then it was gone. Barley might have imagined it.

Although Rye seemed confident that Barley could handle this, Barley didn't think he could. If the ferryman gave the pole to Lord Chiselwart now, with all his soldiers watching, with them ready to strangle Rye at any sign of trouble, there was no way for this to turn out well.

The tired sheep leaned against Barley's leg. The sheep! Barley watched Lord Chiselwart wind the sheep's rope, along with Barley's, securely around his hand. A small idea formed in Barley's head. A way to save Rye. He'd have to be bold, and quick, but maybe it would work.

"Take us across, ferryman," Lord Chiselwart ordered.

The ferryman nodded. As he stuck his pole in the water, he gave Barley a questioning look, droopy white eyebrows up, then shot a glance at Lord Chiselwart. He seemed to be asking if Barley wanted him to hand off his curse to this man.

Barley wanted to shake his head. He didn't want to put Rye in danger. But then he thought about the villages. Crystal Springs was only a short journey away. He couldn't let this army attack them. And what would happen if Lord Chiselwart conquered the Land Far Away and maybe the entire Emerald Realms? As a knight, it was Barley's duty to protect his lands from enemies to the crown. Trembling, he swallowed down his fear and gave the ferryman a stern, steady gaze and a slight nod.

A smile spread across the ferryman's face, and he put his finger to his lips for Barley to be quiet. Then the ferryman slowly raised his pole and planted it, moving the ferry platform about an inch before slowly raising his pole again.

After a few minutes, Lord Chiselwart seemed to notice that the opposite shore wasn't getting much closer. "Hurry up!" he shouted at the ferryman. "Can't you go any faster?"

"Your horse is so heavy, and my old bones are so tired," the ferryman said.

"I have five hundred men who need to cross this river!" Lord Chiselwart bellowed. "At this rate, it will take all night!"

"Patience, your lordship," the ferryman said in a slow, tired voice.

"Give me that pole! I'll show you how it's done!" Lord Chiselwart climbed down from his horse. "Hold these until we're across." He shoved his horse's reins and the ropes at the ferryman's chest and then jerked the pole out of the ferryman's hand.

Huffing and grunting, Lord Chiselwart plunged the pole into the river again and again. The ferry moved faster over the water. In only a few minutes, they would be across.

Taking the reins and the ropes, the ferryman moved to stand with his back to the soldiers on the riverbank and Barley directly in front of him. Barley felt the ferryman cut the ropes from Barley's wrists and from his neck. Lord Chiselwart was so busy pushing the ferry along that he didn't notice.

Barley gave the ferryman a grateful nod and then reached for the rope that held the sheep. The ferryman put it in Barley's hand, and Barley put his hands behind his back again.

The ferry jerked to a stop that made Barley stumble forward. Lord Chiselwart had run the platform hard into the opposite bank. "There. Now see if you can't go a little faster on your way back to the other side." He held the pole out to the ferryman.

Instead of taking the pole, the ferryman stepped off the ferry with Barley, the sheep, and the horse. As soon as the ferryman's foot touched the shore, he straightened up. "It is you who will be going back to the other side," the ferryman said to Lord Chiselwart in a surprisingly strong voice.

Lord Chiselwart turned around and began pushing the ferry platform toward his waiting army. "What? What's happening?" he shouted. "Help! I've been tricked! Help me! Kill the prisoner! Now! Someone help me!"

With his heart pounding so fast he thought it would burst, Barley took the sheep and dashed with it to the top of the riverbank, high enough that all of Lord Chiselwart's army could see. "*Ring tickle rit rickle,*" he whispered in the sheep's ear as he raked his fingers through its wool. A shower of gold coins clinked onto the riverbank.

At the sound of the gold, the army on the other bank of the river fell silent.

"Look!" Barley shouted. "I've got the sheep that makes the gold, and if any of you want to get paid, you'll let my brother go!"

The soldiers on the far side of the bank seemed uncertain. The one holding Rye glanced between Barley and the struggling, shouting Lord Chiselwart as if he wasn't sure what to do. Rye had his eyes shut, his head leaning to one side, with the rope tight around his throat. His chest jerked as he fought to draw breath.

"Don't listen to that boy!" Chiselwart shouted, huffing as his arms worked the pole. "Help! Help me! I can't stop!"

"Listen to Sir Barley," the ferryman called out, and Barley could believe that he had once been a king. "The sheep is rightfully his and his brother's."

Watching his brother being choked filled Barley with unbearable love and anger. Like a shaft of fire rising through him, Barley's whole body surged with a certainty, an authority, that he had never felt before. "Let my brother go!" he commanded.

The soldier holding the rope around Rye's neck let go. Rye dropped to his knees, gasping. His head bowed, and his dark hair nearly touched the ground.

"Chiselwart has a new occupation, as you can see," Barley said. "So I will be taking charge of this army now as a Knight of the Land Far Away. You are all to stay on that side of the river and await further orders, but free my brother from his bonds and let him come across."

THREE

The new ferryman complained all the way across the river and shouted some very nasty things at Rye when Rye boarded the ferry. Rye did his best to ignore him, staying as far from him as the small wooden platform would allow. As soon as the ferry neared the other side, Rye jumped off into the shallows and waded to the bank.

"Barley, you were amazing," Rye said as he wrapped his arms around his brother. "I don't think I could have done that. Those men, they just . . . did what you said."

"There is a great leader in you, Sir Barley." The old ferryman, who was a ferryman no more, put his hand on Barley's shoulder. "If you will accept my services, I will be pleased to help you negotiate some new terms of employment with the captains of the army."

Rye found the magic tablecloth in one of Chiselwart's saddlebags and then sat quietly to listen to the negotiations. In spite of Barley's young age, Rye thought his brother seemed in equal company with army captains and former kings. Rye smiled to think of how Barley had saved him all by himself. No magic sword, no magic petals—just something magnificent that had come over Barley and made him unquestionably in charge. Rye knew for certain now that Barley was ready to watch over Humble Village without his help. The only question was how to convince Barley of it.

FOUR

Sir Barley Fields rode home at the head of an army of five hundred men, along with a magic sheep, a magic tablecloth, his brother Rye, and an old man who had once been a king. As they passed the Lost Forest Inn, Barley waved to Willem, who was raking autumn leaves in the yard. "How do you like my army?" Barley called.

"It's very nice," Willem said, his eyes wide and confused. "Is that what you've been doing these last few months? Raising an army? There was a selkie boy here looking for you not a week after you were here the last time. Oh, I see you've found your sheep."

"What's this?" The shutters of an upstairs window banged open, and the minstrel poked his head out. "An army? And is that the ferryman?"

"His name is Matthias," Barley said.

"Did he remember who he was?" the minstrel asked.

"No," Matthias, the retired ferryman, said with a carefree laugh. "I simply like the name."

"This looks like it would make a good song! What's the story, Sir Barley?" the minstrel asked.

"No time now!" Barley said. "We have to hurry and free our friend from the dungeon of my castle. If you see Fennly again, tell him he can find us at home."

FIVE

Barley was counting on Grafton Chiselwart's brigands being the same lazy, good-for-nothings that they'd been at Lost Castle. It turned out he was absolutely right. Confident that Chiselwart would return triumphant, the brigands hadn't even set a watch of their own, but had lounged around the castle, expecting the army to protect them. The brigands were taken completely by surprise when the entire army turned against them, drove them out of the castle, and chased them into Grayfallow Swamp. While the army managed the brigands, Barley and Rye ran down to the dungeons with the captain of the castle guard, who opened the dungeon and freed Janet Grover from her cell.

"Barley!" Janet squealed, and pounced on him with a hug. "You're all right!" She stepped back, blushing. Then her smile dropped away, her eyes on Barley's neck. "Oh, no. What happened?"

"Nothing. It's fine," Barley said as he self-consciously rubbed at one of the scabs left over from the rope.

Janet grabbed Rye by the hand and towed him into the cell. "Come look at your dragon."

Curled up in a cloth nest that Janet had made from her shawl, the coppery little dragon raised its head and blinked at Rye. It trilled when Rye touched the scales under its chin.

"I've been calling her Cinder," Janet said. "Because she almost didn't make it, nearly went out like a cinder, but then it turned out that she still had some fire in her. You can call her something else, though, if you want."

"Cinder is a good name." Rye gently scooped up the shawl with the baby dragon inside it.

Six

It wasn't long before Cinder was well enough to ride on Rye's shoulder. She perched there, her emerald-green eyes bright and curious, as Rye tipped a bucketful of nix into the millpond. When the last of the water had been poured out, along with a few pieces of gold, the nix lifted his head above the surface. He considered the young willows planted on the shore, the mossy mill wheel with its sad, creaky moan, and then looked down at the faint sparkle of gold in the darkness beneath the water. With a sound like the chuckle of a brook splashing among stones, he pulled his lips in a wild, happy grin, stuck his tongue out at Rye, and leaped all the way out of the water before diving down and disappearing.

On the banks of the pond, the people of Humble Town clapped and cheered. It was Humble Town now. It had grown too large to be a village. Barley had dismissed most of the army with generous discharge pay and only kept enough men to safely guard his castle and his town. But with all the new homes for the remaining soldiers, plus the families of the castle workmen who had decided to stay, Barley's castle now overlooked many tidy rows of cottages.

"Feast at the castle tonight to celebrate the reopening of the town well," Barley called out. "Everyone's invited. Be there at sundown."

"Can I move my shop back to where it was now?" Nat Smith asked as he slapped Barley on the shoulder. "Or do I have to keep it by the well?"

"Yes, you can move it back, and thank you for your help," Barley said.

The townsfolk moved off, talking among themselves. Matthias laughed with Soldier Jack over something the old soldier had said, and Mother Baker could be heard sternly warning her children never to go near the millpond again. Barley stood with Rye and watched them.

"We should put up a fence," Barley said. "And a sign. Draw a horrible picture of the nix poking his sharp-toothed face out of the water to warn everyone away."

Rye took a deep breath. "Barley, I've been thinking." Now that the nix was taken care of, he felt it was time for him to go. "Prince Aster said if I went to King's Town . . ." he trailed off, hoping Barley would understand what he was trying to say.

"I've been thinking too." Barley turned to face him, his blue eyes serious. "I want you to go, Rye. I mean, I don't *want* you to go. Of course I'll miss you, but I want you to go because I know you want to." Barley turned his gaze out over the river. "I've been thinking that Wizard Thornberry was right about the way those petals worked. It's just that I didn't know until now that there are different kinds of true love. When Willem's sister gave up talking so she could break his curse, and then when he forgave her for making a mistake and leaving him with that wing, that was true love. And when you were willing to let the parataxis eat you to give me a chance to get away from it . . ." Barley had to stop for a moment and rub something out of his eye.

Rye nodded, warm inside with knowing that Barley did understand. "Or when someone you care about is in trouble, and you find the strength to help them."

"Yes," Barley said. "And there's another kind of true love. It's the kind where you let someone go, even though it's going to be sad for a while."

"I'll come back," Rye promised. "In a few years when I'm a knight. Or maybe in a few weeks, if King Hugric thinks saving his son from a parataxis was a noble enough deed."

"What grand times we'll have then," Barley said with a big, eager smile. "We'll go adventuring together all up and down the kingdom."

Rye smiled too, but something didn't feel quite right.

SEVEN

"Take good care of Cinder for me," Rye said to Barley a few days later as they stood together where the path to the castle gate met the road.

"Of course." Barley leaned back as the little dragon wriggled in his hands, flapping her one good wing and trying to get to Rye.

"You have to stay, Cinder," Rye said. "Squires don't have time to take care of pet dragons."

The little dragon sagged like a wet stocking.

"Goodbye, Rye," Mother said, giving him a tight hug. "We know you'll make a fine knight."

"Just like your brother," Father said with a proud smile. He clapped an arm over Rye's shoulder.

Rye's heart sank a tiny bit. He told himself it was because he was going to miss his parents. With a deep breath and a long sigh, he took one last look at the castle that stood over his village home. He checked the strap of his pack. He checked the magic sword the fairy had given him, safe in a new leather scabbard his mother had made. Then there wasn't anything left to check. "I'd best be going," Rye said.

The people of Humble Town called out their farewells. Rye waved to them and then turned north toward the bridge. It had been a beautiful fall day like this, only a year ago, that Wizard Thornberry had stopped in the road on his way home to Wizard's Keep and asked Barley how he'd earned a knight's sword.

Rye took a step to the north, toward King's Town, and then stopped. He spun around in the road and faced south instead.

"Barley, give me that dragon," Rye said.

"Rye?" Barley asked.

"Humble Castle already has a knight," Rye said. He laughed at himself for taking so long to see it. "A very fine one too. What it needs now is a wizard."

"No!" Barley said, but he was grinning. "You scoundrel. How dare you betray me like this?" He let the dragon jump onto Rye's outstretched hand.

"Farewell, Sir Barley, until we meet again!" Rye bowed as the dragon ran along his arm and settled on his shoulder. "I'm off to Wizard's Keep to be apprenticed."

"A wizard?" Rye's mother sounded surprised, but pleased. "Oh, won't that be useful?"

"Whoever heard of a wizard with a sword?" Barley asked.

"Who says I can't be the first?" Rye asked, walking backward as he held up his hands and shrugged.

"Stay out of trouble!" Barley called. "If you don't, I'll know it!"

"Same goes for you, brother!" Rye patted the magic sword at his side, waved one last time to everyone, then headed down the road to Wizard's Keep.

Bear this humble tale away free. May it ring the world and come back to me.

Please leave me a review!

If you enjoyed this book, take a minute to leave a review on Amazon or Goodreads. Thank you! I can't wait to see what you have to say!

More adventures to come in
Barley and Rye 3: The Wizard of Frogsmire

ABOUT THE AUTHOR

In third grade, Rebecca J. Carlson wrote her very first story, in which a girl builds her own spaceship, flies to a distant planet, and saves an alien race from a tyrannical gold-eating monster. She's been concocting tales of imagination and adventure ever since.

Visit rebeccajcarlson.com or stop by facebook.com/rjhcarlson and say hi. She'd love to hear from you!